Once Upon a Disaster

Holly Copella

To Uncle Neil
& Aunt Lisa Morris

ACKNOWLEDGMENTS

Copella Books: First Paperback Edition 2017
Printed by CreateSpace, An Amazon.com Company
Cover Artist: Daniela Owergoor
Dani-owergoor.deviantart.com

PUBLISHER'S NOTE

Chapter One

A man in his late twenties fell against the wall while clutching his bleeding, bruised cheek. He could barely stand on his feet while cowering before his attacker. Griffin uncertainly lifted his eyes and looked at the man standing over him. Cody Riley wiped the blood from the pearl-handled grip of his semiautomatic handgun onto a handkerchief while eyeing the injured man, who now panted. Cody was an imposing figure, standing over six-foot-two. The man in his mid-twenties wasn't excessively muscular, but his bleached white moderately spiky hair gave him the appearance of someone sinister. Cody *was* sinister. Griffin remained hunched against the wall with his hands out defensively in front of him, possibly expecting to be shot by the same gun that just struck him.

"It was a mistake," Griffin chirped with fear. "It won't happen again. Give me another chance."

Cody aimed the gun at Griffin's head, causing him to cry out with horror. As Cody's finger tightened on the trigger, Griffin trembled with fear.

"Let's not be too hasty, Cody," a man announced from the nearby shadows.

Griffin now looked toward the man appearing for the first time since he was tossed into the basement corridor of the old apartment building. The man in his mid-thirties, wearing an expensive suit, paused several feet away from the potential crime scene. Jared Carmichael had a look that instantly screamed mob boss. His thinning hair was slicked back with expensive hair products, his fingernails professionally manicured, and he wore a permanent creepy grin chiseled on his face. A younger generation of Mafia, Jared lacked any sort of ethics from previous generations.

"You stole from me," Jared announced with a firm glare. "That's not something I tolerate from any of my employees." He then hesitated. "Even lowly club bartenders such as yourself." Jared seemed to consider the situation. "You're young and impulsive, I get it," he remarked as a strange grin crossed his face. "I'm willing to forgive the money you've stolen from me. We'll consider it a down payment on a job I'd like you to do for me."

"A job?" Griffin suddenly asked then appeared relieved as well as enthusiastic and managed a nervous laugh. "Yeah, sure. Anything. You name it."

"This afternoon, I want you to meet some colleagues at the Strafford Hotel on Main Street," Jared announced. "Come in the back way through the parking garage to avoid the bellman. Be there at noon. Room 1020. Tell them I sent you. You follow their instructions, and we'll call it even."

"Strafford at noon," Griffin announced. "Room 1020. I'll be there. Thank you, Mr. Carmichael."

Jared casually waved him off with little interest. "I abhor morning killings anyway." He gave the man a firm glare. "Don't be late," he warned.

"I won't," Griffin replied.

§

The Strafford Hotel was the ritziest hotel within the small city. It was the only place in town with a valet and a doorman. The twelve-story building was one of the tallest, although considered small compared to most hotels in larger cities. Griffin entered the hotel through the parking garage as instructed, to avoid being seen by the doorman. He rode the elevator up to the tenth floor and promptly arrived at room 1020 at noon with seconds to spare. Griffin gently tapped on the door, which was immediately opened, allowing him to enter.

Griffin stepped into the lavish suite containing a sitting room, wet bar, and the bedroom off to the side. He barely glanced at the man standing alongside the door as he looked around the suite, his eyes falling upon the breathtaking view from the massive wall of windows. As the door shut, Griffin turned to the man who had let him inside. A hulking man, Bernard, stared down at him and nodded toward the bedroom.

"In there," the man announced.

Bernard lacked emotion as well as personality. He wasn't too hard on the eyes, but there wasn't a lot going on inside his head either. He wore his dark hair pulled back in a four-inch ponytail, making his head look bigger than it already had looked. Griffin now appeared suspicious. He hesitated then reluctantly headed toward the open doorway before the bedroom. He stepped into the doorway and saw Cody waiting inside the bedroom. Griffin's eyes immediately strayed to the king-sized bed where a woman lay naked beneath the sheets. He stared at the woman a moment before realizing she was unconscious or worse. He eyed Cody alongside him.

"Is she--?"

"This is how it's going down," Cody firmly instructed without bothering to reassure him of the woman's condition. "We need leverage with another client. You're going to strip down, get into bed with her, and I'm going to take a few dirty pictures as insurance."

"Just get into bed with her," he announced. "Nothing else, right?"

Cody chuckled in his throat, humored by the question. "Still pictures, idiot," he announced. "We aren't doing a porn video. Just cuddle the lady and let us take our pictures, so we can get out of here before she wakes."

Griffin nodded with less conviction and did as the man instructed. He was about to leave his briefs on, but Cody insisted they come off too. It was an odd request, although the entire situation was an odd request. Griffin did as he was told, climbed into bed with the unconscious woman, and cozied up to her motionless body. He breathed a sigh of relief that her body was, in fact, warm, indicating she was still alive. Cody snapped at least twenty digital pictures with his cell phone, instructing Griffin how to hold the woman and what expressions he wanted him to make. On a few, Cody had to reposition the woman's arm or head to help sell the shot. It was over in less than fifteen minutes. Cody fiddled with his cell phone then eyed Griffin.

"We're done here," Cody announced while standing near Griffin's pile of clothes. He placed his cell phone in his inner jacket pocket and eyed the man sitting beneath the sheets. "Get your ass dressed and take off. Take the parking garage entrance. Same as before."

Griffin tossed the sheet off him and was about to climb out of the bed when Cody lunged forward and punched him twice in the face, sending him back onto the bed. He hit him a third time, knocking him unconscious.

Chapter Two

The accounting firm of Wesson and Wesson was on the far end of town in a small industrial park located alongside several seedy looking businesses. Most of the businesses were either for sale or already out of business. The city hoped that the property would be bought by the city or big businesses, which would bring prosperity to their town.

It was a little after 12:30 P.M. Amanda Quinn and Russ Thomas sat at the large table in the conference room with a husband and wife client. They were discussing the future of the couple's company and how Wesson and Wesson could help their business grow. Amanda was an attractive woman in her mid-thirties with dark hair and a make-up free face. She was nearly as beautiful as she was smart. Russ was a few years older than Amanda. He was neither handsome nor unattractive. He was average height and build with less than memorable features. Amanda had done most of the talking, pitching their accounting firm to their potential clients. When she finished, it was Russ' turn to close the deal. Russ was just about to speak when his phone vibrated on the table. He glanced at it and was about to push the silent button when something caught his attention.

Amanda stared with silent surprise as Russ picked up the phone and pushed a button without even excusing himself. His face drained of color a moment then became bright red as his eyes narrowed with a look resembling anger. He barely managed a polite smile as he bolted up from his seat.

"Excuse me," he announced while stepping away from the table. "There's been a family emergency." He looked at Amanda. "I have to go."

Before she could question or protest his hasty departure, Russ hurried from the conference room, leaving her alone with their clients. Amanda stared after him with some surprise then managed a smile and looked back at the couple.

"I'm sure everything is okay," she informed them. "Why don't I just finish our proposal myself?"

The couple finally took their eyes off the door after Russ' hasty departure and managed a smile then nodded.

§

Russ' dark sedan raced up to the Strafford Hotel and barely slowed before the valet stand. He didn't even hand his keys to the startled young man, who awaited orders to park the car. Russ ran for the front door, where the doorman barely had time to open the door for the angry man. The doorman and valet exchanged strange looks, uncertain what to make of what had just happened. The doorman shrugged.

Once inside, Russ ran through the lobby in a whirlwind, shoved his way onto the elevator, and repeatedly hit number ten. There were three people on the elevator with him. His look of mayhem concerned them, considering the way they darted looks at the angry young man. On the first stop, all three passengers left the elevator, even though someone had obviously pushed the eighth floor. Russ shifted from foot-to-foot within the elevator, impatiently awaiting the tenth floor.

When the elevator reached his floor, he bolted through the open doors and headed down the corridor. He briefly glanced at his cell phone then paused before room number 1020. Russ promptly pounded on the door. When there was no response, he pounded a little louder. Several doors on the tenth floor opened, allowing other guests to peer into the corridor to check on the commotion. The door finally opened. Russ bolted into the room, prepared to fight the first person he saw. When he turned toward the man who had opened the door, Bernard punched him several times in the face until he fell to the floor unconscious.

*G*riffin slowly woke with some disorientation. He was still naked beneath the covers in the king-sized bed alongside the young woman. He felt his aching face then looked at the woman lying beside him. Blood soaked through the white sheet and her face was ghostly pale. Griffin cried out while springing upward into a sitting position. As he looked across the room, he saw Cody casually seated in the chair alongside the bedroom door. Cody stood with little reaction, removed a semiautomatic containing a silencer from his hidden shoulder holster, and aimed it at Griffin. Griffin put his hands in the air defensively and attempted to protest. Cody pulled the trigger twice, firing two nearly silent shots into Griffin's bare chest. Griffin collapsed to the bed, wheezed several times, and then expelled his last breath. Cody casually left the bedroom and ran into Bernard in the living room. Bernard picked up Russ' unconscious body and carried him into the bedroom.

Cody exchanged magazines in his gun and removed the silencer, placing both in his pocket. The big man held Russ up as Cody placed the gun into his limp hand. A pillow was already positioned over a large potted plant. Cody assisted Russ' finger into pulling the trigger, firing the gun twice through the pillow nearly a foot away and into the potted plant. The thick dirt prevented the bullet from ripping through the pot, and the pillow kept the dirt from flying out. The goal was to have other guests hear the shots fired without leaving traces of four additional bullet holes. He waited only a second before firing another two shots. Bernard dropped Russ' body with the gun still in his hand while Cody grabbed the bullet-riddled pillow and swiftly collected the discarded bullet casings. Bernard grabbed the potted plant, leaving behind an untouched plant similar to the one he carried. Both hurried from the bedroom and across the living room to the connecting door. They entered the connecting guestroom and locked the door behind them.

Russ slowly woke on the bedroom floor and pulled himself to his feet. He saw his wife and an unfamiliar man lying dead in bed together. For a moment, he was unable to move. He then saw the gun on the floor near his feet. Russ twitched then ran from the room. As he entered the hallway, he heard the fire doors opening and several voices. Russ ran down the corridor. More sounds of commotion were heard coming from the second fire stairs. Russ looked around, saw the linen closet, and then bolted inside. He braced the door shut and attempted to sort out what had just happened. He looked around the linen closet.

A maid's cell phone was on the nearby cart. He grabbed the cell phone, punched in a number, and frantically typed on the small keypad. As he pressed the send button, someone attempted to open the linen closet door. Russ tossed the cell phone into the bin with the dirty linen then turned to face the door as it was thrown open. Two security guards stood in the doorway with their guns aimed at him.

"Freeze!"

Chapter Three

It was nearly 1:30 P.M. Amanda sat behind her desk with her head in her hand while pounding on keys on her keyboard with the other. She was obviously annoyed with Russ for running out of their important meeting the way he had. It was now unclear whether or not they would get the big account. Her sister and brother-in-law trusted her with the account, and now it could be lost. Her cell phone vibrated across her desk. She glanced at the unknown number indicating a text message and chose to ignore it. Half an hour had passed, and Amanda's mood hadn't improved any. She groaned and allowed her head to fall against the desktop. There was a commotion in the hallway, causing her to glance toward her open door. Her sister, who was also her boss, poked her head into her office. Mandy was only a year or two older than Amanda, but they could almost pass for twins.

"Did you hear about Russ?" Mandy gasped with wide, horror-filled eyes.

Amanda stared at her with surprise and possible alarm. "Russ? No, what happened?"

"It's all over the news," Mandy announced. "He caught his wife in bed with another man and shot them both."

Amanda gasped while staring at her sister in disbelief. "Is that the text message he got during our meeting?"

"I wasn't even aware he'd left," Mandy remarked with some surprise. "He tried to run from the police and fell from the roof of the Strafford Hotel."

"Oh, my God!"

"I know," Mandy cried out then cringed. "That hotel has twelve floors!"

A strange look crossed Amanda's face as she stared at her sister. "His wife was with another man?" she almost demanded. "I don't believe it."

"They were killed in bed together," Mandy informed her. "Not much room for doubt, I'm afraid."

"She'd never cheat on him," Amanda remarked almost more to herself.

"It's on the news in the breakroom," Mandy announced then hurried from the office.

Amanda sat back in her chair and sank into thought. She then eyed her cell phone, considered something, and snatched it from the desk. She checked the text message from the unknown number. Amanda suddenly shot up from her chair.

"Oh, my God," she gasped then ran from the office.

Amanda avoided those heading into the breakroom to sneak a peek at the news report of Russ' double homicide and suicide then hurried into his office. She ran to his desk, tossed herself into his chair, and felt underneath the desk. She removed the flash drive from its hidden location then placed it down the front of her shirt as she stood and shoved her phone in her pocket. She hurried from Russ' office before anyone would see her then joined the others in the breakroom.

Despite the commotion in the Strafford Hotel's tenth-floor corridor, Cody and the hulking man relaxed on the sofa watching television. Both appeared moderately bored, but leaving didn't seem to be an option. Bernard flipped through channels without staying on one program longer than a few seconds. Cody rested his temple on his fist and glared at the big man.

"Can you just find something and leave it there?" Cody remarked.

"There's nothing on," Bernard balked.

Cody groaned and put his hand over his eyes. "You're worse than a two-year-old."

There was a knock on the door, alerting Bernard. Cody motioned for him to relax then stood and approached the door. He peered through the peek hole then unlocked and opened the door. A police officer in his late thirties stood rigid in the doorway and stared at Cody with a stern look.

"I'd like to talk to you about anything you may have heard next door," the officer announced firmly. "May I come in?"

Cody stepped away from the door. As the officer entered, he shut the door behind him. The officer turned to face Cody then frowned and shook his head.

"We've got a problem," Officer Newman announced.

Cody's eyes narrowed. "What sort of problem?"

Officer Newman removed a cell phone from his pocket. "I saw traces of blood outside the linen closet," he announced. "When I searched the closet, I found this inside a cart of dirty linen." He pressed a button and showed him the last text message sent. The rushed text message from Russ said, "I'm innocent. Carmichael framed me. Important information on flash drive in desk. Take to FBI. Police on mob payroll. Trust no one!"

Cody suddenly sneered then slammed his palm against the nearby wall table. "Who did he send it to?"

"We're not sure," Officer Newman replied. "I'm having one of our guys at the station check into it. We should have a name in a few hours."

"It's obviously someone at the office," Cody informed him. "He must have accessed some incriminating information from Carmichael's computer and downloaded it onto a flash drive. Whoever received this message may already have found the flash drive."

"We searched the office last night and his house this morning when we nabbed his wife," Officer Newman informed him. "We didn't find any flash drive."

"Obviously there's one out there somewhere. We need to know who he sent this to," Cody demanded. "Find out now!"

A man in his early thirties dressed in a poor man's business suit entered the accounting office a little before three o'clock in the afternoon. His raggedy tan trench coat immediately brought to mind a bumbling television detective. He approached the front desk and flashed his badge.

"I'm Detective Miller with homicide," he announced in a moderately gruff tone. "Is the owner available? I'd like to ask some questions about one of your employees."

For a man of his age, Detective Miller looked hardened and not particularly friendly. He kept his light, curly brown hair short and neat. He stood a tick below average but had a stocky build that made him seem bigger than his actual height.

"Russ?" the receptionist immediately gasped.

"News travels fast," Miller muttered then looked around. "I'd also like to look around his office, if no one has any objections."

"Josh and Mandy are in the breakroom with the rest of the staff," the receptionist informed him sadly. "It's been a stressful afternoon on all of us."

"I'm sure it has," Detective Miller replied, seeming to lack compassion, although he was dealing with a double homicide-suicide. At least the perpetrator taking a swan dive from the rooftop closed his case in a hurry.

"I'll show you to the breakroom," the receptionist announced while standing. It was obvious she didn't like the young detective already. "I don't think they'd have any objections if you wanted to look around Russ' office, but you'll have to ask them about that."

As Detective Miller followed the receptionist down the corridor, Amanda stood within her office doorway, her arms folded insecurely across her chest, as she watched him pass. She was obviously conflicted about the contents of the flash drive. The text from Russ said not to trust the police. He specifically instructed her to give it to the FBI. She watched the detective pass with mild suspicion. Which police officers were working for the Mafia? How many of them couldn't be trusted? She shivered at the thought.

Chapter Four

It was nearly four o'clock that afternoon, and the office would be closing in another two hours. Josh and Mandy excused the employees who wanted to leave early due to the devastating news. Functioning as if everything were normal after what they'd learned was difficult. Amanda remained in her office and got very little done herself. She would have loved to leave early, but she always rode in with her sister and Josh. Her husband, being the wonderful man he was, offered to come and get her early if she wanted to go home under the circumstances, but she declined his offer. She needed time to think about her situation and the flash drive.

Despite nothing unusual happening around the office, she felt uneasy almost as if she were being watched. It was ridiculous! The detective was gone after thoroughly searching Russ' office, and no one else had arrived since then. The text was sent from someone else's phone, which meant if Russ was telling the truth, anyone chasing him wouldn't have known he'd contacted her.

She spent much of the afternoon pacing her office since most of the employees had gone home, so there was no one around to see her subconscious pacing. Amanda turned and was startled to see a fifteen-year-old girl standing in the partially open doorway to her office. She jumped causing the girl to raise her brows with a curious look.

"Jumpy today, Aunt Amanda?" the teenager remarked.

Amanda stared at her teenage niece a moment with surprise. "Jade?" she practically gasped. "I thought you were away at spy camp."

Jade laughed at the comment. "Yeah, it's not spy camp," she remarked then groaned. "I wish it were. It's so lame there. I thought it'd be like junior police training, but it's more like cheerleading camp. I had to get away from all the games and campfires."

Jade had her mother and aunt's girl-next-door beauty. She would grow into a beautiful, independent woman. Perhaps a little too independent.

Amanda stared at the teen a moment longer, uncertain how to respond. "Jade, that camp is twenty miles from here," she remarked. "How did you get here?"

"It was only a two-hour hike through the woods," Jade replied without care then shrugged. "I caught a bus once I reached the four corners."

"Do your parents know you slipped away from camp?" Amanda suddenly demanded and folded her arms across her chest. "They're going to kill you if they find out."

"No, they don't know," Jade firmly replied then raised an arrogant brow. "I was hoping you'd be the understanding aunt and not tell them either."

Amanda groaned and sat on the edge of her desk. "So I'm just supposed to forget you popped into my office? Don't you think Judy at the front desk will tell them?"

"Nope," Jade replied while grinning. "I slipped in the back entrance."

She eyed her young niece. "The back entrance? That door is locked."

"Yeah, code lock," Jade replied. "You don't think I know the code? Believe me; I don't want to get caught skipping camp. My parents will freak."

"And you came to me just to implicate me in your crime?" Amanda remarked while smirking.

"No, not exactly."

Amanda stared at Jade a moment then chuckled softly. "You need money."

"Bingo," Jade chirped while hiding her smile. "Just enough to grab some dinner, catch a movie, and for the bus back to four corners. I'll be back at the camp before dark."

Amanda straightened while groaning and headed for her purse, which was in the closet hanging beneath her favorite black, leather jacket. "And what about when the counselors ask where you've been all day?"

"Nature walk," Jade replied a little too eagerly while flashing a smile. "And it'll be the truth."

Amanda rolled her eyes to keep from laughing. She removed some money from her wallet then stared at her leather jacket a moment with her back to Jade.

"So no one knows you're here?" she reconfirmed.

"No one but you," Jade replied. "Don't let me catch you squealing on me. I'll have a badge one day, and I'm not beyond giving you a ticket."

Amanda removed the flash drive from the front of her shirt and stared at it a moment. She looked back at her jacket hanging in the closet.

"I won't tell a soul, just so you don't tell on me either," she replied without looking back at the young girl. "Make sure no one sees you leaving."

"Not a problem."

Amanda reached inside the inner pocket of her leather jacket and easily ripped the thin liner. She slipped the flash drive through the small rip, allowing it to fall between the liner and outer layer of the leather jacket. It would remain safely somewhere around the bottom of the jacket until she could later retrieve it. Amanda removed the jacket from the closet and turned to face Jade. She handed her forty dollars and the jacket.

"Take the jacket," she firmly insisted. "By the time you're in the woods this evening, it's going to be chilly."

Jade accepted the jacket but was more interested in the large amount of cash she was being handed.

"Forty dollars?" Jade gasped with surprise then beamed at Amanda. "Thanks, Aunt Amanda."

"Just remember," she warned. "No one can know you were here. If your parents find out you skipped out on camp, and I knew about it, they'll never let me live it down." Amanda then pointed a warning finger at her. "And I want my jacket back when you come home on the weekend. Don't lose it. You know that's my favorite jacket."

"I know. It was the first gift Uncle Rafael bought you when you were dating. I promise I won't lose it," she announced then happily hugged her aunt while grinning. "Thanks, Aunt Amanda."

Amanda returned the hug a little longer than necessary. She pulled away and somehow felt oddly uncomfortable while looking at the teenager.

"I love you," Amanda announced.

Jade smiled at her aunt while slipping into the jacket. "I love you too, Aunt Amanda."

She watched the girl slip from her office then sat on the edge of the desk, deep in thought.

Chapter Five

Six o'clock finally arrived, and Amanda was happy to get out of the building. Mandy and Josh were chattering endlessly about the incident with Russ that afternoon. They didn't stop from the time they left the building until they were driving in the car. Amanda remained silent and pre-occupied the entire time. She needed to find a safe location to call the FBI and have them secretly meet her somewhere to hand them the flash drive once she retrieved her jacket from Jade. Although their drive was only twenty minutes from the office to their homes on the outskirts of the small city, it felt like a lifetime in the car. Mandy glanced into the back seat and looked at her sister.

"Didn't you hear me?" Mandy asked.

Amanda looked at Mandy with a clueless expression. "No, I'm sorry," she replied, unable to shake her fears. "I must have been daydreaming."

Amanda glanced through the back window and noticed a black car the same color as theirs behind them. As they made a turn, she saw the car make the same turn. She knew she was being ridiculous. No one knew Russ sent her that text. No one could possibly know she found the flash drive. As they approached the winding road heading uphill, Amanda kept an eye on the car behind them. It seemed to be getting a little closer. Josh looked in his rearview mirror and must have been thinking the same thing. Amanda tensed in the seat. It was just a coincidence. They took the final curve and headed back down the hillside on a similar, winding road. The black car suddenly raced up behind them, causing Josh to shout out with frustration.

"Idiot!"

The car attempted to pass them on the winding back road, startling all three.

"What the hell is he doing?" Mandy cried out. "He's going to get someone killed!"

The black car drove alongside their car and suddenly veered into their lane, ramming their car's front end. The car swerved off the road and struck the guardrail. Josh attempted to brake while cursing out the driver. Mandy screamed while clinging to the door handle as she watched sparks fly from the metal guardrail scraping her side of the car.

"Don't stop!" Amanda cried out from the back seat. "He's trying to force you off the road. It's not an accident!"

Whether Josh believed her or not, he took his foot off the brake and gave the car more gas. The aggressive car raced alongside them, attempting to get in front of them, while Josh tried to keep ahead of the evil driver. The car got alongside them and just a little past their front end before ramming into them with added vigor. Their car plowed through the metal guardrail and flew down the embankment several yards before crashing to the bottom. Despite their seatbelts and airbags, all three were jolted harshly within the car. Once the car came to a stop, Amanda opened her eyes and looked around with disorientation. The car was turned partially onto its side, although she was sure they had flipped several times. She could see Josh and Mandy in the front seat. Neither were moving, but she couldn't tell if they were still breathing. Amanda frantically attempted to remove her seatbelt to check on her sister and brother-in-law, but it wouldn't budge. To her surprise, the rear door was pulled open with a hideous creak of metal grinding metal. She looked at the man by the open car door and held back her startled gasp.

Cody stood over her a moment then saw her purse on the floor by her feet. He grabbed her discarded bag, routed through it, and removed a flash drive. Amanda remained silent while staring at him. He offered a chilling grin then shut the car door. Amanda groaned softly and shut her eyes. She then heard a strange sound. As her eyes opened, she saw flames racing along the line of gas toward the car. Cody stood near the start of the flames, maintained his chilling grin, and then gave her a friendly sort of wave before heading back up the embankment. The car burst into flames. Amanda could be heard screaming from the backseat as the car was engulfed in fire. The car suddenly exploded.

Chapter Six

Rain poured down over the large group of mourners within the cemetery. There was a sea of black umbrellas surrounding Amanda's shiny casket covered in a blanket of fresh flowers. The words of the reverend were barely heard above the pouring rain. A short, mousy looking man in his mid-thirties, wearing a new, black suit now soaked by the rain, stood before the grave without an umbrella. He stared at the flower-covered casket with a fixated, glossed over look in his eyes. Despite the attempts of others to help shield him with their umbrellas, Rafael Quinn was drenched. Jade stood on the other side of her aunt's casket and stared at Rafael. It was hard to tell if she felt sorrow or pity for him. She found it difficult to take her eyes off him throughout the inaudible ceremony. His wife, Jade's beloved Aunt Amanda, was dead. She knew little about her uncle, despite his being married to her aunt for over ten years. He was a private person, preferring to suffer today in silence. Perhaps, they were more alike than she thought.

It was one week after the funeral and things were far from getting back to normal, particularly for fifteen-year-old Jade. A moderately worn car pulled up to the once charming, little home located in the small development. The lawn and landscaping, which was once immaculate now showed signs from nearly two weeks of neglect. Jade got out of the car wearing the black leather jacket her aunt had loaned her that day. She inhaled deeply and then released a groan while staring at the little house. Jade didn't want to be there, but no amount of whining or protesting was going to change her fate. The female social worker soon joined her and handed her the worn duffel bag. The tired, overworked social worker managed a tiny smile but obviously felt sorry for the teenager as she escorted her to the house.

"The rest of your personal belongings will be shipped here later this week," the woman informed her. "I assume your family attorney told you about the house, the business, and the rest of your parents' assets."

"Yeah," Jade replied with a bored sigh. "Once sale on the house and office is final, the proceeds will go into escrow along with the insurance money until I turn eighteen. It's not fair. I already have a house, and the insurance money is more than enough to support me for a few years. I shouldn't have to live with someone else."

"You're fifteen," the social worker firmly reminded her then muttered, "Going on twenty-five. You can't live on your own at fifteen. Someone has to take responsibility for you."

Jade hated being told that over and over. The legal system sucked. They walked onto the porch and paused before the door. Before the social worker had a chance to knock, Jade turned toward her and made another plea for mercy.

"Couldn't I just stay with my friend?" Jade asked in a somewhat whining tone. She hated being reduced to whining. She promised herself she wouldn't go that route. It just wasn't fair. "Her mother really likes me."

"We've been over this before, Jade," the social worker announced sympathetically. "She's a single mother living in a cramped apartment with three children. Even though she's willing to take you in, we just can't approve her." She hesitated then indicated the door before them. "He's your uncle, and he agreed to take you in."

"He's not my uncle," Jade pouted, turning her head away from the woman alongside her. "He's just the odd, little man my aunt married." She groaned and allowed her shoulders to sag with defeat. "He's a reclusive workaholic. In the ten years he was married to my aunt, I'd only met him a dozen times." She then made a face and reflected back on their few interactions over the last decade. "He's creepy."

"It's only temporary, Jade," the social worker assured her. "I know how hard this has been on you; losing your parents and your aunt in that car crash, but he's hurting too." She managed a warm smile. "Just try to get along for a few weeks until we can find something more permanent."

Her words hit hard. Jade hadn't actually thought about her uncle's pain. After all, he lost his wife in the same crash. She frowned and nodded. The social worker rang the bell. There was a long, silent wait. Both fidgeted slightly at the lack of response. The door finally opened to reveal Rafael Quinn. Although his usually neat brown hair was slightly mussed, he was meticulously dressed and clean-shaven. Unfortunately, he maintained the same distant look in his eyes from the funeral. He stared at them a moment and seemed almost puzzled by their presence. Despite attending all three funerals, Jade wondered if he even recognized her.

"Oh, was that today?" he asked timidly and without emotion. "It must have slipped my mind."

Jade eyed the social worker and sharply raised her brow as if giving her a firm 'I told you so'. The social worker offered a tiny smile and nudged her into the house.

§

The next two days passed incredibly slow, offering zero adjustments between the unlikely duo. The small, immaculate study was filled with antique furniture and didn't appear to have a paper out of place. The entire house was the same way, without as much as a dust bunny out of place. Rafael sat in the chair behind the expensive desk and stared blankly at the computer with the same glossed over expression in his eyes while holding his head in his hand. He was supposed to be working, but he hadn't moved since he sat down several hours ago. There was a faint knock on the closed door. Rafael didn't move nor look up.

"Come in," he barely muttered.

The door opened to reveal Jade. She looked around the tidy study then focused her attention on the man behind the desk. He remained in his trance and didn't bother looking at her. She drew a deep breath and attempted to be pleasant. He seemed unable to function after losing his wife, making Jade wonder how he survived before they'd been married.

"I made dinner," she announced in the most cheerful voice she could manage under the circumstances.

"Uh, huh--" Rafael muttered, clearly not hearing a word she said.

She stared at him a moment longer, waiting for a reaction. "Are you going to have some?" she finally asked.

"Uh, huh--"

Jade groaned, shook her head, and left, shutting the door behind her.

Chapter Seven

Three days later. The once immaculate living room decorated with antique furnishings now had cracker crumbs spread along the floor in front of the sofa. Jade lay upside down on the antique sofa with her feet dangling over the back and her head hanging down to the floor. She munched on crackers while talking on her cell phone with her friend, Lily, in dramatic boredom.

"Well, it's sort of like living alone," she explained to her friend, "except there's only one bathroom and sometimes he's in there for an hour or more."

"Doing what?" her friend squawked.

"Making himself pretty," Jade remarked then groaned. "How should I know? He just sits and stares at his computer all day." She then considered her comment. "Well, sometimes he sits and stares at the kitchen table. I'm not even sure if he's eaten anything since I've arrived, and the bills are piling up on the hall table. He hasn't even opened them. I'm considering writing out the bills myself and forging his signature." She lost a cracker to the floor but didn't bother picking it up. "Lord knows he'll never know the difference. He rarely says a word, but at least he smells good."

"Think you should call someone?" Lily asked.

"Who? Neither of us has any family, and I doubt he has any friends," she remarked while frowning. "He's supposed to be self-employed. Computer repairman or something, but he certainly hasn't done any sort of work since I've been here. He never leaves the house."

Rafael passed by the living room with his head down and the same lifeless expression on his face. A moment passed. He reappeared in the living room doorway and stared at Jade draped across the expensive antique couch. His mouth fell open as he pointed at the floor.

"Are those crumbs?" Rafael suddenly demanded.

Jade glanced at Rafael from her upside down view, startled having heard his voice for the first time. "Oh, my God! It speaks," she gasped into the phone. "I'll call you back." Jade sprang upright on the sofa and looked at him with mild surprise. She extended the sleeve of crackers. "They're crackers. Want some?"

"They're crumbs, and I'll ask you to pick them up," he boldly cried out.

She stared at him with some surprise and hid the devious smile that followed. "Oh?" she enquired slyly. "Does the mess bother you?"

"Yes, it does."

Jade faked a serious look with added drama. "Then you may not want to look in the kitchen."

Rafael appeared bewildered then concerned and hurried down the hall. Jade smiled and casually stood. She pivoted on the balls of her feet a moment and waited.

"What happened to my kitchen?" he cried out from across the house.

"He's obviously never met a teenager before," she remarked then grinned slyly. "This could be fun."

Jade casually leaned in the kitchen doorway and ate more crackers, purposely making crumbs, while watching Rafael scrub the stove with cleaning gloves and a sponge. He cleaned like a madman possessed by a demon. She found it rather amusing. It was the most life she'd seen from the man.

"I'm making spaghetti tonight," she announced cheerfully with a mouthful of crackers while spitting out crumbs as she spoke. "Will you be joining me for dinner?"

Rafael stopped scrubbing and turned to look at her with horror on his face. "You've done enough damage to my kitchen already," he informed her. "If you want spaghetti, I'll make it."

"Suit yourself," she replied with little emotion then straightened. "I'll just get started on the laundry."

Jade was about to turn and leave the kitchen with her pack of crackers.

Rafael quickly turned and stared after her. "I don't want you touching the laundry."

She turned back around and immediately hid her humored smile. Jade's look was once again serious. "Should I start on the bills then?" she asked while pointing toward the hallway. "There are quite a few of them on the hall table."

"No, I'll take care of them," he retorted and returned to scrubbing the stove. "You just go clean those crumbs you made." He stopped and spun to face her. "I want you to strip the linens from your bed and put your dirty clothing in the laundry basket." He returned to the stove. "If you're staying in my house, you're not going to run around in wrinkled clothing like that."

"As you wish." Jade turned and left the kitchen with a satisfied smile. She'd finally found Rafael's 'on' switch. Perhaps his self-pity days were over.

§

*T*wo days later. Jade sat on the sofa, her feet tucked under her, and her laptop set up on the coffee table. Her frilly blonde friend, Lily, was visible on the computer screen while they talked to each other face-to-face. Jade propped her temple to her fist while giving her friend a dreary look.

"I think I liked him better when he just sat around all day and stared at things," Jade remarked with a groan.

"What's he doing now?" Lily asked.

"Cleaning *everything*," Jade announced. "He spends an hour in the bathroom primping, another hour cleaning up after himself, and another hour cleaning the bathroom after I've showered. I think he's going Norman Bates 'Psycho' or something."

"He's grieving," Lily responded with little reaction. "Right now he's in denial."

"No, he's nesting," Jade corrected and sat up straight. "The only time he speaks to me now is to tell me what needs to be cleaned. When I do clean, he ends up cleaning up after I've cleaned. There's no pleasing the guy."

Rafael entered the living room with his duster and dusted the furniture without acknowledging Jade. He glanced at the computer screen as he passed the back of the sofa. He suddenly paused and looked at Lily on the computer screen. Lily looked back at him, smiled cheerfully, and waved.

"Hi, Mr. Quinn," she chirped with enthusiasm.

Rafael stared at the monitor and appeared stunned at what he saw. "Oh, my God--"

"It's Skype," Jade cheerfully explained, guessing he was unfamiliar with the concept.

"Look at the state of that bedroom," he suddenly cried out. "You need to do some serious cleaning, young lady!"

Lily looked back at Jade with disbelief. "Hmm, I see what you mean."

Chapter Eight

Five days later. Jade lay across her bed on her stomach with her laptop in front of her, talking with Lily. She was clearly upset as she wiped the tears from her face while Lily watched her friend with a concerned look.

"Is it that bad?"

"I've been here almost two weeks," Jade informed her while sniffing. "If it weren't for his compulsive cleaning, he wouldn't even talk to me. It's worse than being invisible." She became animated while sitting up and hugging her pillow to her chest. "I lost three people I loved in that car accident. He lost one." She tossed her pillow aside with a combination of sorrow and rage. "I can't take it anymore. He's not the only one grieving. Just because I don't show it--" Jade again wiped her tears.

Lily watched her from the computer screen and appeared frustrated. "Of course you can stay with me," her friend replied. "You know my mother would love to have you."

"I doubt he'll even notice I'm gone," Jade snapped with anger then sniffed again. "At least it'll be one less person for him to clean up after." She attempted to compose herself. "I'll throw my bag together and be over in an hour."

"It's midnight. That's quite a walk to my place," Lily remarked with concern. "Tomorrow is Saturday. My mother can come get you in the morning."

"No, I'm not staying here one more night," Jade insisted. "I'll be fine. I can take care of myself."

"I hear that," Lily remarked while scratching her brow. "I'll wait up for you."

"See you in an hour."

Jade shut her computer and jumped off the bed. As she frantically searched for her bag in the messy closet, she heard a thump from downstairs. She hesitated a moment then looked at her bedroom door. Another thump followed, definitely coming from downstairs. She was immediately curious by the unfamiliar sound, especially so late at night. As his usual pattern, Rafael was in bed by ten o'clock. She approached the bedroom door and left her room. Jade silently walked down the stairs and paused at the bottom to listen. The house was mostly dark except for a light on in the kitchen and the study. She was about to approach the study and check on Rafael when she heard another thump followed by grunts coming from the living room.

"Where is it?" a gruff male voice commanded.

Rafael sounded panicked while responding. "I told you, I don't know what you're talking about."

Jade listened only a moment before quietly approaching the living room archway. She looked into the living room and saw Rafael tied to one of his antique armchairs. His face was bruised and bleeding while an unfamiliar, moderately repulsive looking man stood over him and flexed his sore right hand.

"I can do this all night, Quinn," the intruder, Snyder, casually informed him. "We want that information. We know you have it."

"I can't tell you what I don't--"

Rafael saw Jade standing in the living room archway, and his expression suddenly dropped. Snyder turned as well and saw her. Jade gasped when she saw the evil expression on the man's hardened face.

"Run!" Rafael shouted.

Jade turned from the living room archway and ran for the front door. She attempted to open it, but it was dead bolted. As she reached for the deadbolt, she could hear the man shouting behind her, indicating she'd ran out of time.

"Get her!"

Jade looked back and saw two intruders, Flint and Carson, emerge from the study. Snyder stood in the doorway and indicated the girl by the front door. The two younger men spotted her and pointed before charging down the hallway for her. Jade gave up on the deadbolt, gasped at how fast they were moving toward her, and bolted up the nearby stairs as her only escape. Both intruders chased her, being a little slower on the stairs than the spry teenager. Snyder returned to the living room and smiled deviously as he approached Rafael, who remained transfixed and horrified while listening to the thundering feet running along the second floor practically above his head. The sound was almost deafening.

"And here I thought you were all alone," Snyder announced then chuckled. "Our evening just got a little easier and possibly a little more interesting."

"Leave her alone!"

Snyder maintained his evil grin. "Oh, we will. If you tell us what we want to know." He then casually shrugged. "If you don't, the little girl is going to get herself a few new boyfriends."

They could still hear the sound of thumping feet running upstairs. Rafael looked at the ceiling and remained horrified while attempting to follow the sounds. He looked back at Snyder.

"Leave her alone," he cried out in fear that quickly turned to rage, "or so help me, I'll kill you!"

Snyder suddenly laughed and casually looked at the dirt under his fingernails with mild disinterest in the threat. "If I only had a dime for every time I'd heard that--"

Chapter Nine

Jade ran into her bedroom and attempted to slam the door behind her. Flint shoved the door open with amazing force, tossing her across the room. She spun around near her bed to face her attacker and attempted to weigh her options in the split second that followed. Before she had a chance to react, he tackled her to the bed. Jade screamed and struggled against his hands as the large man attempted to subdue her. Her heart was pounding as she fought against the man, possibly fighting for her life.

Carson appeared in the bedroom doorway, practically out of breath. "You got her?"

Flint grinned deviously while pinning her to the bed. "Yeah, I've got her," he announced with a low chuckle. "Give me a minute to tenderize her before I bring her down."

Carson shook his head in disgust. "Make it quick."

Once Carson left the room, Flint looked at Jade beneath him while keeping her wrists pinned to the bed. The large man weighed heavily upon her, nearly suffocating her beneath him. She stared into his eyes as if reading his thoughts and stopped struggling, wasting precious energy.

"And here I thought tonight was going to be boring," Flint teased.

Jade gasped with surprise and horror as he kissed her harshly on the mouth.

§

Rafael fought against the duct tape binding his wrists to the arms of the antique chair in a frantic attempt to free himself. They heard someone coming down the stairs, alarming him. As Carson entered the room, thumping sounds indicating a massive struggle was taking place on the second floor above them. Snyder glared at Carson, silently demanding a response.

"He'll bring her down in a minute," Carson informed his partner.

Rafael stared at the ceiling while listening to the sounds as his expression shattered. Anger and rage crossed his face as he slowly lowered his eyes and glared at Snyder.

Snyder met his gaze then grinned and shrugged. "What can I say? He enjoys his work."

Rafael stared at the man with an unpredictable look in his eyes. "I'm going to kill you," he snarled in a tone never used by the docile man before.

Snyder laughed, mocking his rage. "Yeah, I've heard that before from guys a lot tougher than you," he replied then casually shrugged. "Not that any of them are alive to tell about it."

The thumping finally stopped.

Snyder chuckled and looked at his watch. "Wow, that's fast even for him." He grinned at Rafael, attempting to enrage him further, although it wasn't necessary. "He likes them young."

Rafael stared at him with a cold, hateful look. Snyder stared back at him, but Rafael didn't look away. Snyder's jovial expression mocked him.

"Now, do you tell us what we want to know, or does she get to know the rest of us just as intimately?" Snyder teased.

"I am going to kill you," Rafael again snarled.

Snyder stared at Rafael a moment then punched him in the face. Rafael spit out blood then slowly turned his head back to him. His expression remained unchanged and nearly psychotic.

Snyder straightened at Rafael's reaction then frowned and turned to Carson. "Go get them," he ordered. "Bring the girl down here. He needs more convincing."

Carson nodded and left the room heading for the stairs.

Snyder leaned down and looked Rafael in the eyes. "Maybe you'll be more cooperative when we do that little girl in front of you."

Rafael didn't take his eyes off him as his fingernails dug deep grooves into the antique wood of the armchair.

§

*C*arson entered Jade's dark bedroom and looked at the mussed, empty bed. He looked around the empty, silent room for either his partner or the teenager. When he didn't find Flint or Jade, he appeared bewildered.

"Flint?"

Something thumped from the bedroom next door. Carson left Jade's bedroom and entered the dimly lit master bedroom one room over. The bed was neatly made and there wasn't an object out of place. He looked around then approached the closet without hesitation, removed a gun from his shoulder holster, and threw open the louver door. Jade cowered on the floor with a frightened look on her face while clinging to her aunt's leather jacket she now wore. She had blood on the corner of her mouth, some blood on her shirt, and bruises on her wrist. He smirked and, with his gun, motioned her out of the closet.

"Gave him the slip, huh?" Carson teased.

Jade sobbed softly and timidly crept out of the closet with her arms folded insecurely across her abdomen while clinging to her jacket.

He pushed her toward the door and laughed as he called out. "Hey, I found your girlfriend. Let's go!"

Chapter Ten

Carson shoved Jade into the living room. She stumbled several feet before catching her balance then turned to face Snyder as tears streaked her face. Rafael stared at the brutalized teenager with a look of horror. He was no longer angry; he was frightened.

"Please, I barely even know this man," Jade insisted with a quiver in her voice while fighting her tears. "He's just the guy who married my aunt. I have nothing to do with whatever you want from him." She cast a look of loathing at him. "He doesn't even care about me."

Snyder laughed while looking at Rafael. "Teenage girls can be amazingly devoted, don't you think?" He looked back at Jade. "Sorry, baby. He's already expressed his feelings for you, which naturally means we have to hurt you to get what we want from him."

Snyder eyed Carson and nodded to Jade. Carson returned his semiautomatic to his shoulder holster, grabbed Jade by her already bruised wrists, and pulled her against him. She braced her hands against his chest but seemed to have no fight left in her. Snyder approached Rafael and smiled deviously.

"Are you going to tell us what we want?" Snyder asked then indicated his man with Jade. "Or does this get messy?"

Rafael now appeared horrified while staring at Jade being held against the intruder. "I'll tell you," he cried out. "Please, just let her go."

"See, you can be cooperative," Snyder announced then eyed Carson. "Do it."

Carson clutched Jade's right wrist and grabbed for her pants with his free hand.

Rafael appeared horrified as he struggled against the chair. "No!"

Jade caught the man's wrist with her free hand, stopping him from grabbing her pants. He looked up with surprise at her fast reflexes and met her gaze. The look in her eyes was cold and emotionless as she locked eyes with the man.

"You shouldn't touch what isn't yours," she hissed in a frightening tone.

Carson's expression was confused and somewhat startled. She violently twisted his arm, causing him to scream, and then kicked him in the side. As he released her, she kicked him in the abdomen. When he doubled over, she spun into a roundhouse kick and struck him in the face. He dropped to the floor with a thud. Jade threw herself to the floor, snatched the gun from his shoulder holster, and rolled into a crouched position, aiming the gun at Snyder. Despite his surprise, he leaped behind Rafael and held his gun to her uncle's head.

"Put the gun down, or he dies!"

Jade slowly straightened while keeping the gun trained on Snyder. Her expression didn't soften. There was no longer any sign of the helpless teenage girl.

"Do you think I care?" she snarled. "This isn't my fight. I just want to leave."

Carson slowly moved to his feet not far from Jade. Without even flinching, Jade removed a second gun from the back of her pants, hidden beneath the leather jacket, and aimed it at Carson. He jumped with surprise and stared at the gun pointed at his face. She kept a gun on each man but kept her eyes trained on the man behind Rafael. All three men, including Rafael, stared at the second gun with surprise. Jade noted the question in their eyes then offered a tiny smile while indicating the gun aimed at Carson.

"This?" she asked and snorted a soft laugh. "Oh, I got this off your *dead* friend upstairs. He got all up in my personal space." Her look again turned serious. "I'm going to leave now. The first person who so much as flinches as I head out that door will be eating a bullet. Is that understood?"

All three men appeared stunned while staring at her. Jade slowly took a step backward toward the archway with guns trained on both men.

"We understand," Snyder replied while attempting to act casual, but he was obviously stunned at what he was witnessing. "Of course you're free to go. No hard feelings, okay?"

Jade slowly turned her head toward Carson, who stood between her and the doorway. The moment her head was turned, Snyder removed his gun from Rafael's head and aimed it at her. Jade barely even looked at him as she pulled the trigger, shooting him twice in the chest. Carson seized the opportunity and lunged for Jade. She immediately returned her attention to him and squeezed the trigger, shooting him in the upper abdomen. As he dropped to the floor near her feet, Jade slowly straightened and frowned.

"Damn it," she cursed softly. "My aim sucks!"

Jade placed one of the guns down the back of her pants and hurried to Rafael where he remained tied to the chair with a stunned expression on his face. She removed the duct tape from his wrists and the arm of the chair. They heard sirens in the near distance from her earlier call to the police. Once he was freed, Rafael jumped up from the chair and pulled her into his arms. She tensed with surprise. When he didn't release her, she uncertainly returned the embrace.

"Don't get all emotional on me now," she remarked softly, choking on her words.

Rafael pulled back just far enough to look at her face and gently touched her bleeding mouth. His look was tender yet frightened. "Are you okay?"

Jade laughed softly, mocking her injuries. "You should see the other guy."

"Did he--?"

There was a moment of silence at the perceived question. It took Jade a moment to realize what he was trying to ask. She eyed Rafael and pulled away from him with a look of horror and disgust.

"Ewe--no!"

"I--I don't understand. How could you--?" Rafael stared at her and shook his head. "The kicks; the shooting."

"Maybe if you took time to actually talk to me, you would know I'm a black belt in karate," she remarked matter-of-factly. "I've been taking lessons since I was five. I want to be the best, ass-kicking police officer this town has ever seen." She shook her head while frowning her disapproval. "It's hard to believe you're supposed to be some sort of genius. You haven't exactly impressed me these last two weeks."

Rafael appeared stunned then turned docile. "I'm sorry--" He pulled her back into his arms and clung to her as if he'd never let go.

"I'm so sorry, Jade. When I thought he'd hurt you--" He held back his sobs. "I could never live with myself if something happened to you. You're all I have left in the world," he practically sobbed. "I can't lose you too."

Jade uncertainly returned the embrace and smiled gently while fighting her tears. "Yeah, well, maybe I'll give you another chance."

Rafael laughed softly and clung to her, almost smothering her. Jade finally pulled away and stared at him.

"Why didn't you just give them what they wanted instead of letting them beat the crap out of you?" she finally asked.

He groaned softly and ran his fingers through his short hair. "It's not that easy," he replied. "I believe they wanted my computer program idea, but it hasn't been put down on paper yet." He indicated his head. "It's still up here."

She shook her head. "Yeah, you're a genius all right."

Chapter Eleven

Ten years later. The area surrounding the building which was formerly Wesson and Wesson Accountants had grown into the business district of the city's dreams. The entire area had been bought, torn down, and rebuilt into the successful cluster of booming businesses. A taller building not far from the old accounting building seemed to be the mecca of the entire area. Virtual Play Programmers encompassed two floors of the ten-story building in the business district of the small city. The building itself was owned by Virtual Play, Ltd., but many of the suites were rented to other businesses. The programming company utilized the ninth and tenth floors, the tenth floor contained offices for the big shots. The ninth floor was home to computer programmers and executives who made the gaming company the success it was.

Beyond the modern ninth floor lobby and receptionist desk, the open floor plan contained large cubicles, nicknamed 'cubicle square', with over two dozen men and women milling around the main floor. It seemed as if they were socializing, but some of the games were a team effort with much collaborating. A conference room, breakroom, and enclosed offices lined the walls on either side of the cubicles. The overall atmosphere was fun with larger than life icons from their most successful games hanging from the walls as well as some life-sized statues of popular characters.

The receptionist's large, semi-circular desk contained a large wall behind it to keep those within the lobby from seeing what went on behind the scenes in cubicle square, which generally included a lot of joking and horsing around. With the nature of the company, fun time and employee interaction was encouraged to keep its employees creative. An attractive woman in her late twenties with shoulder-length auburn hair sat behind the receptionist desk and busily worked on her computer. Despite the company's casual policy, Dani Phillips usually wore dresses and high heels. She wanted to look professional for their important clients' first impressions. As she busily worked, the phone rang. She picked up the phone without missing a keystroke.

"Virtual Play Programmers," she announced into the phone and finally stopped typing. "How may I help you?" She listened to the response and remained outwardly cheerful. "Certainly. I'll connect you with Greg."

Dani pressed several buttons then hung up. She immediately returned to her computer, typed something, then sat back and smiled. A close-up of her computer screen revealed she was sending instant messages to someone named 'Boyd'. Two secretaries appeared from cubicle square and approached the receptionist desk within the lobby. Abby and Janice also dressed up for their jobs just because they enjoyed wearing pretty clothes. Their eye-candy appearance was misleading as both women were good at their jobs. Both women were in their late twenties to early thirties. Abby had light blonde hair that went past her shoulders when she wore it down, while Janice was a natural strawberry blonde. She usually wore her hair up, since it was so long, it nearly touched her waist. Despite the women having to strain behind Dani's desk, they managed to catch a glimpse of her computer screen. Dani shielded her screen from her friends' prying eyes and smiled politely.

"Is it lunchtime already?" Dani asked.

"If you can tear yourself away from Boyd, you can join us," Abby knowingly teased.

"I brought lunch today, but thanks anyway."

Janice casually leaned against the tall front of Dani's desk and shook her head. "You've been talking to this guy for months," she remarked. "When do you intend to actually meet him?"

"I kind of prefer this to the real relationships I've had," Dani replied while leaning back in her chair then indicated her screen. "This, ladies, is the perfect man. And as long as I never meet him, he'll stay that way."

Abby frowned and shook her head. "Wow, Greg really screwed you up, didn't he?"

"It wasn't Greg's fault," Dani replied with little regard to her past relationship. "I knew it'd never work. Taking up with him was just poor judgment on my part."

"Come on, come to lunch with us," Janice practically whined. "We can trash men. It'll be fun."

"Not today, but thanks."

Both women reluctantly left their friend to her 'work'. Dani eagerly returned to her computer.

Dani IM: *"Sorry--friends asked about lunch. Told them I had a date. LOL."*

Boyd IM: *"Really? Where are we going?"*

Dani laughed softly at Boyd's boyish charm. Although they'd never met and she had no idea what he even looked like, she enjoyed his witty personality. He'd never asked to see a photo of her and never offered to send one of himself. She'd meant what she said to her friends. An internet relationship was all she could handle at the moment. The sting of the real dating scene was a bit much these days. What she said was true. In her mind, Boyd was perfect, and she preferred to keep him that way for now.

Chapter Twelve

Mostly everyone had left by five o'clock, but the hardcore programmers typically hung around until closer to six o'clock. Creating computer games was an art form, and the programmers were the artists. Artists sacrificed themselves for the sake of their art. It was noble, in a way, but it also kept Dani late almost every evening. She couldn't exactly complain, at least since she'd been corresponding with Boyd in marketing. She didn't have a home computer, so she had to limit their conversations to work. As the last of the programmers headed out for the day, with a heavy heart, Dani typed her final message to Boyd.

Dani IM: *"Heading out.   Chat tomorrow?"*

Boyd IM: *"See you 'wink' tomorrow."*

Dani couldn't contain her grin. She loved Boyd's charm and talking with him brightened her mostly dull days. She logged off just as a man in his early thirties approached the desk. Greg Martin was a lanky, well-dressed man who had more charm than actual good looks. It had been months since she and Greg called it quits. It wasn't as if their relationship had been a lengthy one. She became disenchanted with him only a few weeks into the relationship. He wasn't nearly as open and honest as he seemed around the office. She always felt he kept a large part of his life hidden. Although she couldn't be certain, she often wondered if it were alcohol or drug related. Greg looked around and appeared curious.

"Is it just us?"

"Yeah, mostly everyone scattered a little after five today," she replied.

"Why don't I walk you out?" he suggested. "That parking garage gets creepy after hours."

Dani stood and took in an eyeful of him, wondering what she ever saw in him in the first place. "Sure, I'll protect you," she teased. "Don't worry."

"Aren't you cute--" Greg smirked without humor. "No wonder we broke up."

He was obviously still bitter about their breakup. She did end things a bit abruptly after his strange behavior got the best of her. Greg glanced toward the back beyond the cubicles and appeared curious at something he saw.

"Is someone in the copy room?"

"The repairman stopped by, but that was an hour ago," she replied. "Maybe he left the light on."

Greg suddenly grinned and suggestively raised his brows. "Maybe it's someone fooling around after hours," he teased. "Wait here. I'll check it out."

Greg walked past the cubicles and headed toward the back of the main floor. Dani removed her purse from the bottom drawer, opened it, and found her car keys in anticipation of Greg's return. After a few minutes had passed, she started to worry when Greg didn't return. She stepped around the partition wall and looked beyond the cubicles. The copy room was now dark, but there was a light on in Greg's office, which seemed odd. Dani appeared curious then set her purse down on top of the desk and approached his partially open door.

As she paused in the doorway, she saw Greg sprawled out on the floor, face down and motionless. Before she had a chance to check on him, she saw a tall, menacing looking man in his late thirties sitting behind Greg's desk. He was attempting to gain access to his computer. Trent looked up and saw Dani. She gasped as their eyes briefly met. He had the steel cold gaze of a soldier and the powerful body to match. Dani saw all she needed to see in the man's evil eyes. She darted from the office and ran past the cubicles toward her desk. She grabbed her purse while sprinting past her desk, not even slowing. Dani had little choice because Trent was right behind her. She didn't even have time to stop before the elevators directly in front of the lobby. She couldn't afford to wait.

Dani removed her cell phone from her bag while running along the corridor and carelessly discarded her purse. If she were lucky, perhaps he'd stop for her purse and give up chase. No such luck. The frightening man wasn't interested in cash or credit cards. Dani bolted through the fire door and ran down the stairs. Not surprising, she couldn't get any reception on her cell phone in the concrete stairwell. Trent was directly behind her, thundering down the stairs making enough noise to frighten her. She paused before the fire door on the eighth floor but couldn't access it from the stairwell without a card key. She ran down another level to the seventh floor, passed through the fire door without a carded lock and ran along the corridor. Dani tried every office door without barely slowing. They were all locked!

Trent caught up to her, being she was slowed by her attempt to seek refuge in one of the offices, and tackled her to the floor. From their speed and the hard hit, both rolled across the floor. Dani was fortunate enough to end up on top and kneed him in the groin. As he groaned in agony, she scrambled off him, realizing too late that her phone remained on the floor near him. She tried another door and discovered it was unlocked. She darted inside and ran across a gym room of sorts while looking around with panic. She saw a second door on the opposite side and ran across the room for the door. She was halfway to the door when it suddenly opened, alarming her. A security guard appeared in the doorway, forcing her to come to a sliding stop so she wouldn't crash into him.

"Whoa, where's the fire?" the guard, Allen, demanded.

"There's a man chasing me," she shouted while pointing back the way she came.

Allen looked in the direction she pointed, grabbed his nightstick from his belt holster, and without hesitation hurried for the door on the opposite end. Dani couldn't force herself to move, knowing this guard was putting himself in danger to protect her and the building. She wrenched her fingers together while watching him.

"Be careful!"

As Allen opened the door, Trent punched him in the face, sending him back several steps. Allen took the hit surprisingly well for a moderately stocky man and attempted to strike him with the nightstick. Trent caught the stick, easily disarmed him, and struck him with his own stick. Allen fell to the floor and lay motionless from the sole hit. Trent cast the nightstick aside and resumed his pursuit for Dani. Dani panicked and bolted through the second set of doors behind her. She ran into the corridor, sprinted down the hallway, and bolted for the back, fire stairs.

The gym door was thrown open with a loud bang, causing her to look back. She gasped and saw Trent in hot pursuit. As she looked toward the fire door just ahead of her, she noticed the fire alarm pull station. Dani slid to a stop before it and pulled the lever. The alarm wailed loud and shrill. Trent suddenly hesitated, looked around with concern, and listened to the sound of thundering feet in the stairwell. Dani darted into the stairwell with several other people from the eighth floor.

Chapter Thirteen

The following morning, Dani was escorted off the elevator and into the office by a young, part-time security guard. He saw her safely to her desk even though he could have easily stopped at the elevator door and watched her through the wall of glass. Dani was grateful for the added security, but she felt funny receiving so much personalized attention.

"Are you sure Allen is okay?" she asked Ralph as he paused before her desk.

"Allen is fine," Ralph replied cheerfully. "Just a couple of bruises. He'll be back to his old self in no time."

"He was very brave," she informed the guard then considered the comment. "Maybe a little foolish, but very brave."

"He'll be back tomorrow," the guard informed her. "You can tell him that yourself."

Once Ralph left, Abby and Janice hurried toward the receptionist desk. Both women wore concerned looks on their faces and fussed over Dani.

"It's all over the building," Abby gasped while staring at her friend with wide eyes. "Even the coffee guy on the corner heard. Are you okay?"

"That must have been horrible for you," Janice chimed in while half leaning over the taller portion of her desk.

"I'm still a little shaken," Dani replied and felt a little uneasy as she sat behind her desk. Visions of the intruder chasing her from the lobby flashed through her head. She knew she'd never get that man's face from her mind. She drew a deep breath and eyed her friends. "Last I heard the police hadn't caught the guy." Dani hadn't even realized she'd sank into her thoughts. She snapped out of her trance and looked at her friends. "Is Greg coming in?"

"The stubborn fool is already here," Janice informed her while rolling her eyes. Her look then turned serious. "What was the guy after? Who was he? Do you think you prevented him from killing Greg?"

"He said he was the copy machine repairman," Dani informed them then shivered slightly. "Honestly, I thought he left an hour earlier. He must have been lurking around waiting for everyone to leave." She then gave the last question some thought. "I think if he intended to kill Greg, he would have done it right away."

The two women caught a glimpse of a serious looking man in his early fifties stepping out of Greg's office. Janice and Abby recognized the man and scattered as he approached Dani's desk. Larson was one of the company's higher-ups and rarely made visits to the trenches. Despite his age, he was a fairly attractive man with light brown hair containing gray around the temples. He stood tall and had a solid build and sturdy features. For the wealthy executive type, Larson gave the impression he was quite capable of handling himself. He seemed eager to talk with Dani as he paused before her desk.

"Dani, are you okay?" Larson asked with sincerity then almost turned scolding. "You didn't have to come in today. I thought personnel was going to call and tell you to take a few days off with pay."

"They did, Mr. Larson," she replied almost timidly in front of the company big shot, "but I'm fine. I'd rather keep busy and not think about it."

Larson shook his head and sighed. "Yeah, that's what Greg said too," he replied then straightened proudly. "Well, rest assured, we've beefed up security, and we're checking into time locks on the doors so that no one can sneak in after-hours again."

She knew her attacker didn't sneak in after hours, but she didn't feel like correcting one of the company's top brass. "Maybe requiring all repairmen to wear ID wouldn't hurt either."

He snapped his thick fingers and pointed at her. "Excellent suggestion," Larson announced boldly then smiled pleasantly. "There's coffee and doughnuts in the conference room." His look turned serious. "If you need anything, you just call."

"Thank you, Mr. Larson."

She watched with surprise as Larson left through the lobby doors and past the elevators on the other side of the glass wall. Janice and Abby quickly returned to the front desk, surrounding her. Both stared after Larson.

"Wow, a visit from Mr. Larson," Abby announced as her eyes widened. "The big boss himself. He's never even said hello to me." She then leaned against the desk. "Maybe it's just me, but he's pretty damned sexy."

"I wouldn't go that far," Janice remarked then looked back at Dani. "We're taking you to lunch, and we're not taking no for an answer. We'll talk at lunch."

Both women disappeared without waiting for a response on the offer of lunch. Apparently, that was settled. She'd be having lunch with her friends today. Dani sat behind her desk and suddenly felt a strange chill run down her spine. She didn't think last night's incident would affect her as much as it did, but she was suddenly regretting her decision to return to work so soon. A deliveryman entered through the glass lobby doors with a large flower arrangement. She hated to admit she was suspicious of him, but one look at his boyish features convinced her he wasn't there to attack her.

"Delivery for Miss Dani Phillips," he announced.

"That's me," she replied while standing with some uncertainty and stared at the huge flower arrangement.

Dani signed for the flowers, waited for the deliveryman to leave, and then opened the card. It read, *"Hope you're feeling better. Best wishes, President, Virtual Play Programmers"*. Dani opened the envelope that arrived with the flowers. She was surprised to see the five hundred dollar spa gift card. Her eyes immediately widened at the gift.

"Well, thank you, Mr. President," she muttered and withheld her grin. "You can relax, though; I'm not going to sue."

Dani sat at her desk, took a moment to relax, and then logged onto the computer, attempting to sink back into her usual routine to get her mind off last night. She'd no sooner logged on when the instant message began blinking at her. She was a bit surprised to discover Boyd's message sent nearly an hour before her scheduled shift.

Boyd IM: *"Are you okay? Are you there?"*

Dani couldn't believe he'd heard about the incident so fast. She typed into the computer.

Dani IM: *"Bad news travels fast."*

Boyd IM: *"Are you okay?"*
Dani IM: *"I'm fine. Just a little shaken."*
Boyd IM: *"Did they catch the guy?"*
Dani IM: *"No, not yet."*

Chapter Fourteen

Later that morning, Dani continued to work on her computer, gossiping with Boyd when she caught a glimpse of someone entering the lobby. Dani immediately faced forward and gave those entering her undivided attention. A fully-grown Jade Wesson, now in her mid-twenties, entered the lobby with a man following behind by a few lengths. Jade dressed business casual from her white blouse to her black pants and dress boots. The only thing out of place was her worn, black leather jacket. A natural beauty, Jade looked so much like her mother and aunt; she could have passed for their twin sister. As Jade approached the desk, the man alongside her came into view. Despite being a decade older, Detective Miller hadn't changed. He looked almost the same as he had ten years ago, aging gracefully--and possibly a little more cynical. Unfortunately, his shabby suit hadn't aged quite as gracefully. The tan trench coat was in dire need of being retired. As Dani studied the duo, she couldn't think of anyplace the pair would fit in.

"Good morning," Dani announced pleasantly and attempted not to stare at Detective Miller's shabby trench coat. "How may I help you?"

Miller and Jade flashed their detective badges, and Dani suddenly understood why they looked so out of place. Miller, being the senior detective, took control of the situation.

"Miss Phillips, I'm Detective Miller, and this is my partner, Detective Wesson," Miller announced then replaced his badge to his belt. "We'd like to ask you some questions about last night, if you don't mind."

"Is here okay?" she asked while indicating her desk. "The phone's about to start ringing any minute now."

"We won't take up much of your time," Jade informed her while managing a polite smile. "We read your police statement regarding the attack." Jade placed a picture of Trent's mugshot on the desk.

Dani's eyes widened with surprise then horror as her heart pounded and she sprang out of her seat. "That's him! That's the guy," she cried out then looked at the pair of detectives. "Did you catch him?"

"Sort of," Miller replied with little emotion. "He was found dead in an alley not far from here. He'd been dead at least twelve hours. The coroner suspects he was killed within an hour of your attack last night."

"Oh?" Dani remarked while staring at them then fidgeted slightly. "Should I pretend to be upset?"

"We'll understand if you're not," Jade replied with a tiny, knowing smile.

"Do you have any idea what he wanted?" Miller asked while studying her through slightly squinting eyes then cocked his head. "What he may have taken from this office that someone killed him for?"

"I'm sorry. I have no idea what he wanted," Dani informed them. "He must've knocked Greg unconscious and was at his computer when I walked in on him. He was trying to access something, but I don't think he got whatever it was he was looking for. I'm guessing that's why he chased me. He must've thought I could access Greg's computer." She tensed slightly and indicated the cubicles in the area beyond the wall. "Any of our programmers could have something valuable on their computers at any time. Believe it or not, computer game programs are a hot commodity. You'd be surprised how often hackers attempt to infiltrate our systems."

"He wasn't a hacker though, was he?" Miller remarked as if he already knew the answer.

"I've never heard of a hacker making a personal appearance," Dani replied with a serious look on her face. "No, I'm guessing he wasn't a hacker. If you ask me, I don't think he was looking to steal computer games either."

"What makes you say that?" Miller asked with a curious look, although it was obvious he already knew the answer but continued with the game.

"He didn't look like a geek or a genius," Dani announced then considered her comment and gave Miller a strange look. "He looked more like a hired goon."

Miller smirked, almost indicating she'd guessed correctly. "Is Greg Martin here?" he asked.

"I just got here a few minutes ago, but I was told he's here," she replied then nodded beyond her desk into cubicle square. "His office is the third door on the right."

Jade extended her card and managed a polite smile. "If you think of anything at all that might help, give us a call."

Dani accepted the card and watched the detectives head into cubicle square.

§

Jade and Miller sat in the plush, leather chairs before Greg's expensive, executive desk while glancing at the large toys surrounding the room. All were characters from popular games and almost made it seem as if they were within some bizarre computer game. Miller was too serious to appreciate the cartoonish atmosphere of Greg's office. Jade stared at the larger than life characters and had to keep from grinning. Greg appeared less jovial this morning while holding his bruised temple. He eyed the photo and slowly nodded with less enthusiasm than Dani displayed.

"Yeah, that's the guy," Greg informed them then eyed the detectives. "Who is he?"

"His name *was* Trent," Jade announced while keeping her eyes locked on him while awaiting a reaction. "He was an enforcer for the mob."

"Was?" Greg gasped. "You mean he's dead?"

Jade cast a glance at Miller, who strummed his fingers on the arm of the chair. They had both come to the same conclusion but didn't mention it in front of Greg. Ironically, Greg had caught onto the part where the man who attacked him was now dead, but he didn't seem to have any concerns at the mere mention of mob attachment. Was he secretly admitting he knew why he was attacked and his computer hacked?

"Someone put a bullet in the back of his head *execution* style," Miller informed him while raising his brows, driving the Mafia ties home.

Greg finally seemed to catch on and shot up straight in his chair. "Whoa, whoa, whoa," he practically cried out while fidgeting and erratically waving his hands in the air. "A hitman for the mob came after me for something in my computer and gets whacked by another hitman?" He subconsciously rubbed his temple. "Should I be feeling a little paranoid right now?"

"Maybe his boss was upset that he didn't bring back what he came for," Miller suggested in a slightly accusing tone then glared at him without emotion. "So what do you have on your computer that the mob would want?"

Greg immediately tensed. "I write computer games. I'm one pocket protector away from being a nerd," he remarked almost matter-of-factly, although his body language was telling a less convincing tale. "Unless your mob boss is a big gamer, I assure you, I have nothing someone like that would want."

"So nothing pertinent was accessed from your computer?" Jade asked in a moderately unfeeling tone while she studied him.

He was almost more paranoid by Jade's lack of emotion than Miller's hardened attitude. "I think Dani must have interrupted him," Greg quickly replied. "He never got past my password. He must've thought Dani could access it for him."

"I'm afraid we're going to have to ask you to come with us to the station for further questioning," Miller remarked with little emotion, surprising Greg.

"Seriously?" Greg groaned softly and leaned back in his chair while shaking his head. "I should have become a doctor like my mother wanted."

Chapter Fifteen

Dani returned from lunch with her friends, Janice and Abby, just a little after one o'clock in the afternoon. As the women returned to their desks in cubicle square, Dani headed behind her receptionist desk, collapsed into her chair, and immediately logged onto her computer. Her stolen moments with Boyd were the highlight of her day, and she hated missing their lengthy lunchtime talk. She typed on the keyboard announcing her return.

Dani IM: *"Back from lunch."*

Dani sorted mail while waiting for Boyd's timely response. She wasn't sure what his work schedule was, but he always seemed to be available when she needed him. Boyd's whimsical cartoon avatar flashed, alerting her to a new message from her internet boyfriend. She looked at the screen, not surprised by the quick response. She often wondered if he ever left his computer.

Boyd IM: *"Executive lunch? Was getting worried."*

She chuckled softly and typed her response.

Dani IM: *"Friends helped me cross the street. No need to worry."*

Boyd IM: *"I deserved that."*

Dani IM: *"I appreciate your concern--really."*

The main lobby door opened to reveal Rafael Quinn. Now ten years older, he wore small, wire-rimmed glasses, a tasteful suit, and carried a leather briefcase. He fiddled with his cell phone, not paying attention to what was happening around him, and nearly collided with one of the office workers. He barely looked up from his phone and apologized. Dani saw him and immediately snapped to attention. Rafael was one of their computer tech guys, which meant he paid closer attention to everyone else's computer monitors. She quickly typed on the keyboard.

Dani IM: *"Computer repair guy's here. Gotta go."*

Boyd IM: *"The nerdy one with the bad rug or the nerdy one who looks like a Muppet?"*

She held back her humor and smiled at the question. She typed her response.

Dani IM: *"The Muppet--"*

She looked up as Rafael approached her desk still glued to his cell phone. As he paused before her desk, he replaced his phone to his jacket pocket. She was already turned forward facing the desk and giving him her full attention. He offered a timid smile and handed her a service order form.

"Good afternoon, Dani," he announced in a moderately cheerful but timid tone. "The corporate bigwigs want updated firewalls on all the computers. Something about an incident yesterday involving a hacker."

Dani let out a slightly tense laugh while accepting the service form. "Oh, is that what they're calling it?"

He didn't seem to know what she was referencing but let it slide. "If it's okay, I'll start with yours and work my way back. Figure an hour on each unit," he informed her. "If you could give the programmers a heads up on when I'll reach their computers, I'd appreciate it."

Dani logged off on her computer to avoid being caught talking with Boyd, smiled timidly hiding her embarrassment, and moved away from her chair.

"Certainly, Rafael."

Rafael moved behind her desk with her in the moderately tight quarters, briefly eyed the flowers on her desk, and then sat in her chair. He immediately fiddled with her computer.

"Lovely flowers," he remarked without looking up. "Is it your birthday?"

"No, that's a bribe," she teased, knowing he wouldn't get the joke. "I'll tell the others you're here."

Dani squeezed out behind him in her chair, noting his usual pleasant scent. It was a combination of expensive soap, hair products to give his hair that moderately spiky look, and some cologne she had yet to identify. Everyone dreaded Rafael's visits. For a meek, timid guy, he had little trouble scolding the workers when they abused their computer equipment. Dani was both intimidated and intrigued by the odd man, unlike her co-workers who were mostly intimidated and annoyed by him. Dani headed onto the main floor and approached Abby's cubicle first, which was closest to the receptionist desk and probably next on Rafael's route. Janice hurried to join them at Abby's desk, enjoying good gossip.

"I see "Revenge of the Nerds" is back," Janice teased.

"Be nice, Janice," Dani scolded.

"He's a creepy, little guy," Abby remarked with little concern for being nice. "I've actually heard him holding a conversation with the computers. He thinks they're his little patients."

"Hey, I barely know he's there," Dani informed her friends. "As a receptionist, I find that refreshing."

"I agree with Abby," Janice remarked and folded her arms across her chest. "He's creepy. Please tell me he's not here to work on all the computers."

"He is, so plan accordingly."

"Yeah, I'm going to plan my break when he gets to mine, so I don't have to deal with him," Abby muttered. "Did you ever see him with that little keyboard vacuum gizmo? Then he leaves me sticky notes about keeping my keyboard clean. I'm a secretary, not the cleaning lady."

Two of the programmers worked their way closer to the conversation at Abby's cubicle, obviously unhappy with what they were hearing.

"Another update?" Brad muttered then groaned with irritation. "Come on! Those things take forever. How are we supposed to get any work done?"

Brad was the stereotypical computer geek complete with wide-framed glasses and moderately slicked back hair. He was a slender man in his late thirties and wore a t-shirt promoting one of their computer games.

"I don't mind," Peterson remarked. "Gives me a chance to sneak out for an extra cigarette break." He eyed Abby and grinned. "What do you say, Abby? Want to go get coffee when he reaches our computers?"

Abby rolled her eyes. "In your dreams, Peterson," she muttered.

Peterson was a self-proclaimed lady's man. A tall, solid-built man with shoulder length hair and a tanning salon tan, he was moderately impressive to women everywhere but within Virtual Play. The women who worked for the corporation knew Peterson was a womanizer and his suave, caring attitude was a false front for his undesirable personality.

The front desk phone rang, alerting Dani. "There's my phone. Pass the word, would you?"

"Yep, creepy computer guy has arrived," Abby teased then flashed a smile, knowing it bothered Dani.

Dani hurried for her desk in the lobby, joined Rafael behind it despite the close quarters, and answered her phone.

"Virtual Play Programmers," Dani announced into the phone. "How may I help you?" She paused and listened to the caller. "One moment please."

Dani transferred the phone call to one of the offices then tensed slightly from her closeness to the pleasant smelling computer geek. She caught a glimpse of Rafael working on her computer, and it made her unusually tense. Despite shutting down her conversation with Boyd, she didn't like anyone playing with her computer in fear they might stumble upon something she shouldn't have been doing during work hours. She hid her anxiety and casually leaned against the inside of her desk.

"So corporate didn't tell you what happened last night?" she asked, feeling the need to make small talk with the docile man.

She was actually surprised he hadn't gotten the latest gossip. Even Boyd, who didn't work anywhere near the office, heard the news.

Rafael didn't bother looking at her while he worked. "I'm on a need to know basis," he informed her. "They don't feel I need to know."

She subconsciously folded her arms across her chest and held back her shiver. "A man broke into Greg's office and tried to hack into his computer," she informed him. "Beat-up Greg and a security guard."

He hesitated and looked at her with some surprise. His look then turned serious. "No one can hack these computers."

"Really?"

"If they could, they'd be smarter than me," he informed her with little emotion. He returned to his work. "Corporate wants to stop excessive internet usage, so I'll be disconnecting your DSL and deactivating your accounts."

Dani stared at Rafael's profile and appeared horrified at what she'd just been told. "What?" she gasped with surprise while straightening then attempted to cover for her reaction. "I mean, is that necessary?"

Rafael glanced at Dani with a strange look as if awaiting a reason why he shouldn't. She tensed and fidgeted, dropping her hands from her shoulders.

"I don't have a computer at home," she reluctantly informed him. "This is the only place I can check my email."

Rafael casually looked back at the computer and continued to type on the keyboard. "You don't need a computer for that. Just about every cell phone can do that," he casually remarked. "I'm guessing you're more concerned about the hours of daily IMs to Boyd in marketing."

Her heart suddenly pounded as she stared at his profile. "How did you know--?"

"Your computer has no secrets from me," he informed her with little emotion and didn't bother looking at her as he worked. "I'm smart, remember? Your computer retains that information."

Rafael casually leaned back in the chair and pressed a few buttons. Thousands of IMs between her and Boyd suddenly appeared on her screen. Dani appeared horrified and gasped as every message she'd ever sent flashed in front of her.

Rafael finally glanced at her while propping his chin on his knuckles. "Incidentally, which Muppet do you think I resemble? Gonzo or Beeker?"

Dani stared at him, embarrassed that he'd seen that.

He appeared quizzical while raising a clever brow and straightened. "No need to answer that. I'd rather not know," he replied and returned to his work. "All you need to do is go into here and click 'empty'." Rafael clicked the button. Every IM disappeared. "Awe, look at that. Gone without a trace."

"I am so sorry," she gasped while keeping her hand near her mouth as she stared at his profile.

Rafael didn't bother looking at her.

Her entire body stiffened as her heart raced. "Are you going to tell corporate?"

"What happens in the computer; stays in the computer," he casually replied then hesitated and considered the comment. "Actually, that's a falsity. Instant messages can be hacked quite easily." He waved her off without care and returned to his work. "Well, you knew what I meant. Just remember to empty your trash frequently."

"About the internet--?"

Rafael stared at the computer screen and stopped typing. He appeared to consider her question then glanced at her in his usual timid manner. Their eyes met only briefly before he looked away and returned to his work.

"How could I say no to someone who brings me coffee?" he replied.

Dani felt relief sweep through her and managed a smile. "How would you like that coffee?"

"Black is fine, thank you."

Chapter Sixteen

The downtown police station had a historic appeal to it. It had been painstakingly remodeled to fit in with the rest of the historic buildings in the downtown area. Despite the moderately nice area, the small city wasn't without its seedy sections of town. As with any city, they had two or more gangs fighting turf wars over what didn't belong to them, but for the most part, the city maintained a low crime rate. Police officers milled around the station bullpen along with suspects, victims, and the occasional criminal in handcuffs. Although crime was low, that didn't mean it didn't happen. They had their share. Jade was seated at her desk among the dozen or more other desks and worked on her computer. She had plenty of paperwork to catch up on. Like so many of her colleagues, the paperwork was always pushed back until the last minute, and then there was a rush to get it in on time. Her cell phone vibrated on top of her desk with 'Uncle Rafael' appearing on the caller ID screen. Jade immediately answered the phone while casually leaning back in her chair.

"Jade's Porn Palace," she announced in a serious tone. "What's your pleasure?"

There was a long pause. "You know, I really hate when you do that," Rafael muttered from the other end.

She laughed softly while grinning. Pushing her uncle's buttons was a fun and fulfilling pastime. "What's up, Rafael?"

"I'm going to be late tonight."

She smirked knowingly. "Stuck at the office, dear?"

"Corporate wants added security after what happened last night," he informed her. "They're insisting it be done by the end of the day today. Unfortunately, it's going to take me two days."

"What a bunch of pricks you work for," Jade remarked into the phone.

"Yeah, very funny," he scoffed. His tone then turned serious. "I really wanted to talk to you about what happened at Virtual Play last night. Were you still planning on coming over for dinner?"

"I thought you might want to discuss that," she replied simply. "Yes, I was still planning on coming over."

"Good. Would you mind picking up something for dinner?" he asked. "I won't have time to cook."

Jade rocked in her chair while staring at the ceiling and contemplated the request. "I'll make you a deal," she announced while grinning slyly. She could almost hear him groan from the other end. "I'll pick up dinner if you come to my place to eat it."

There was a long, tense pause. "Did you clean?"

"It's clean--ish," she teased and couldn't help but smile.

"I can only imagine," he muttered under his breath. "I'll see you about seven."

"See you then."

Jade disconnected the call, laughed softly, and shook her head. They had a weird relationship, but it worked on every level. Speaking of weird relationships-- Jade saw Miller approach her desk and watched as he tossed a file on top of it near her. She eyed the file then looked at Miller. He always looked so serious, even when he was attempting to be lighthearted and jovial. Fortunately, she knew he liked her, because he certainly had little intention of ever making it known.

"Must I read that or will you give me the short version?" she asked, indicating the file.

"That outstanding citizen is Vahn Lott," Miller informed her with little enthusiasm. "He's a low-life piece of shit transporter for Cody Riley, owner of that dance club on fifth. You know the one. Club Zen."

"Cody Riley?" she asked with surprise. "As in lapdog for mob kingpin, Jared Carmichael?"

"One in the same," Miller replied with little emotion. "It seems our boy, Lott, was seen in the parking garage last night around the time of the break-in at Virtual Play. We have him in room four cooling his heels. He tends to lawyer up at 'hello'." He offered a sly grin. "Want a shot at him?"

She suddenly raised her brows. "Will a 9mm do the trick?" Jade teased.

"Funny."

Jade sprang up from her chair with enthusiasm and snatched the folder. "Sounds like fun."

"Ten bucks says you don't get more than five words out of him before he demands his lawyer."

She grinned proudly. "You're on."

Chapter Seventeen

The small interrogation room was a bland and drab concrete room with little more than a table, four chairs, and a two-way mirror. A ruggedly handsome, neatly dressed man in his early thirties sat casually reclined in his chair behind the desk with his cuffed hands on the table, as he showed no emotion while staring at the two-way mirror. It was possible he was attempting to intimidate whoever was on the other side. Jade entered the room while skimming through his file then eyed Vahn Lott. He didn't bother looking at her and barely acknowledged her presence. Jade made a quick assessment of Cody Riley's newest goon. Vahn was undeniably a powerhouse, indicated by his broad shoulders and muscular chest. With his dark nearly black hair and equally dark eyes, he was undeniably a handsome sight to behold.

Jade was always amazed by how neatly dressed and immaculate hired goons for the mob could be with their appearance. They often smelled as good as they looked. She casually approached the table and tossed the file on top, catching his attention for the first time. He obviously had no intention to cooperate and was playing some sort of intimidation game with her before a word was even spoken. As Vahn eyed her, his expression immediately changed. Anything he had rehearsed seemed to go out the window. He stared at her a moment with a puzzled look and sat straight in his chair.

"Is this a joke?" he demanded, clearly caught off guard by the young, attractive detective sent to interrogate him.

Jade removed a pair of handcuff keys from her pocket and indicated his wrists without a word. Vahn raised his cuffed wrists to her. She casually removed the handcuffs, set them on the table, and took a seat across from him. She didn't take her eyes off him and offered no emotion.

"Is what a joke?"

"Sending in jailbait to interrogate me," he scoffed and again leaned back in his chair, appearing a little too comfortable, while rubbing his wrists. "It's offensive."

"Jailbait?" she remarked while raising a brow then smirked. "I haven't heard that one yet. I'm Detective Wesson, but you can call me Detective Wesson."

He remained silently offended, although not so silent. "Not that this hasn't been fun, but go get your superiors--or daddy. Whoever," Vahn launched. "Tell them they have nothing on me, and they need to release me immediately."

She didn't react to the mild tirade, although she did find it funny that he was bothered by not warranting a seasoned, gritty detective. It must have been quite the ego blow. Ironically, he didn't seem to take offense to the fact that they'd sent a woman to interrogate him. She actually found that moderately refreshing.

"Vahn Lott," she announced while leaning back in her chair. "Transporter for Cody Riley."

"Transporter?" he questioned then chuckled with a humored smile. "No, I'm a chauffeur and glorified messenger boy for Cody Riley. He's a nightclub owner, not a mobster. You people seem to have a difficult time distinguishing between the two."

"Uh, huh," she replied then leaned forward, casually clasping her hands together on the table. "And messenger boys frequently carry 9mm automags?"

He leaned on the table, mirroring her actions and stared into her eyes. "It's a violent world, my dear."

Jade opened the folder, skimmed through some papers, and then made a face while shaking her head. Vahn appeared curious then tilted his head and eyed the folder.

"It says here you've been a bad boy."

Vahn smirked and suddenly turned playful. "If I confess to that, will you spank me?" he teased. "Because I could get into that."

"What was that?" she asked while raising a curious brow. "Sexual harassment of law enforcement?" She shook her head and tossed the folder aside as if moderately bored. "Come on, Lott; don't make this too easy for me."

"Oh, you'd prefer I play hard to get?" he asked then sat back in his chair, his face turning serious. "Okay. I want a lawyer."

"And I want to meet a man who doesn't spout lies with every breath," she replied then cocked her head. "So I guess we're both shit out of luck."

He stared at her with an odd expression, desperately trying to figure her out.

"Security cameras place you in your boss's Bentley at the Virtual Play parking garage last night around the time two employees were assaulted," she informed him.

"I needed a little time to myself, and it seemed like a quiet place to reflect upon life," he casually replied. "If you saw me on security cameras, you must also know I never left the car. I certainly didn't assault anyone."

"Oh, I know you didn't."

Jade tossed Trent's mugshot across the table to him. He barely glanced at the photo and showed no reaction.

"But this man did," she countered while watching him closely. "Do you recognize him?"

"No, I've never seen him before," he replied with no emotion. "Who is he?"

"He's the man chilling in the morgue with a 9mm slug in the back of his skull," she replied without taking her eyes off him, watching for any change in his expression. "Looks like a professional hit."

Vahn's eyes strayed to the picture only a split second, but it was enough for Jade to see a slight reaction. Her callus remark to the man's death caused him to tense, no matter how slight, telling her he knew the man. She also gathered that he either disapproved of the man's murder or didn't know he'd been killed. His lack of emotion returned, and it was back to business as usual.

"I'm not a hitman," he informed her. "You can check my resume."

"Yeah, I have it right here," she announced and again opened the folder. "Several assaults, numerous batteries, a couple of breaking and entering, reckless endangerment with a vehicle, speeding--"

Although she didn't mention it, she found it slightly odd that his police record only went back six months ago. Prior to that, he'd been silently flying below the radar. Twelve years in the military with an honorable discharge and then a few years driving a cab in New York City. Suddenly, he pulls up stakes and moves to their little dark corner of the world where he becomes a transporter for the mob. Something didn't add up.

"But not murder," he informed her of his rap sheet. "I don't kill people."

"Did you drive this man to Virtual Play last night?" she finally asked while indicating Trent's picture.

"No, I've never seen him before."

"I think you did."

"What you think doesn't really matter, does it?" he remarked with little reaction. "Ballistics will show my gun is clean. I haven't fired it in months. I think I've been very cooperative and extremely patient. Admit it. You have nothing on me because I didn't do anything."

Jade studied him a long moment. Vahn stared back at her and showed little reaction, silently attempting to intimidate her. She knew he was lying about knowing Trent and driving him to Virtual Play, but she didn't have any proof. Jade finally sighed and stood, allowing him to win the staring match. She had better things to do with her time.

"You're right, I have nothing on you," she informed him. "You're free to go, but we'll be keeping your gun for testing. If it's clean, you can pick it up later tonight."

Vahn stood with enthusiasm and smiled. "This was fun," he announced cheerfully. "We should do it again sometime."

"Oh, I'm sure we'll be seeing each other again real soon," she countered.

"That sounds promising," he replied then grinned. "Be sure to bring your handcuffs."

She glared at him. "Trust me; I will."

Jade collected the file and opened the door for him. He eyed the door then glanced back at her and offered a charming yet lustful smile.

"Maybe you should give me your number, in case I think of something that might help your case."

"Sure, you can have my number," she replied almost cheerfully. "You'll find my number on the side of every cruiser on your way out."

He leaned against the doorframe and attempted a sexy pose. "You're very hot for a detective."

"Careful, Mr. Lott, you might get shot."

"Is this your idea of foreplay?" he asked while straightening. "Because it's turning me on."

Miller appeared in the doorway with his arms across his chest and stared him down. Vahn eyed Miller then looked back at Jade and smirked.

"Daddy's back," Vahn teased. "We'll have to continue this some other time."

She watched as he casually left the interrogation room. Miller shook his head then handed her ten dollars. She took the money, grinned, and left the room.

Chapter Eighteen

Jade's apartment was located within a decent neighborhood and reflected her tom girl style, although not exactly on budget with a newly hired homicide detective. She had a sizeable inheritance after her parents had died. Between the sale of the house, business, and their combined insurance policies, Jade practically became a millionaire on her eighteenth birthday. Jade had her sights set on buying a house in the future, but she was waiting for one house in particular. Eventually, her parents' house would be for sale again, and then she'd buy it and finally return home. In the meantime, she held off spending most of her money, as she would need it to buy her family home. She did have some nicer used furniture, which was obviously hand-me-downs from her uncle since most had an antique appeal and didn't seem to fit her personality. Jade sat curled on the antique sofa, which had been the same sofa from Rafael's living room. She held a glass of white wine in her hand and remained in her own world. She finally snapped out of her trance.

"And if the day wasn't strange enough already," she continued her mild tirade while gesturing with her wineglass, "Miller let me interrogate this transporter guy."

"Transporter?" Rafael asked from across the room, although out of view.

"Mafia errand boy," she translated so her uncle could follow the conversation. "My first real mob interrogation."

"I don't understand," Rafael announced. "Why do you sound disappointed? Isn't that right up your alley?"

"He was more interested in making eyes at me than playing hardball," she replied with a dreary sigh. "I swear Miller sent me in there just to amuse himself. I mean, the guy didn't even threaten me or anything. It's insulting. A rookie could have interrogated this guy."

Several feet behind her, Rafael stood on a step stool while dusting the light fixtures in his dress shirt, vest, and an apron to protect his clothes. He concentrated on his work and didn't bother looking at her.

"You have a warped idea of a good time, Jade."

She glanced behind her and watched him clean. "Says the man in the apron dusting my light fixtures."

"Cleaning relaxes me," he announced boldly. "What about this business at Virtual Play?"

"Other than the dead guy being a Mafia hitman?" Jade remarked and eyed him.

"A Mafia hitman?" Rafael gasped and stared at her, nearly losing his duster.

She shook her head while staring at him. "Doesn't anyone around there gossip with you?"

"They'd rather gossip about me," he remarked then returned to dusting. "I just found out today that I'm gay."

"Hmm," she responded then sank into her own thoughts while studying him. "That certainly would explain your excessive cleaning habits."

Rafael glared at her, not amused. "I'm not gay," he insisted. "I was very happily married to your aunt for ten years, may I remind you."

Rafael climbed down from the step stool, removed his apron, and joined her on the sofa. He reclaimed his glass of wine and attempted to relax.

"Whatever your man in the morgue wanted was on Greg's computer," Rafael informed her. "Maybe Greg is hiding a little more than you think."

"If he is, he's certainly not giving up that information," she muttered.

"Do you want me to see what's on his computer?" he asked with a curious look.

"No, that would be against the law."

He chuckled in his throat. "Not for me. It's my job, remember?" Rafael reminded her. "Sometimes I think you forget who I am."

She eyed him and raised a suspicious brow. "Do *you* even know?"

"You're so witty, Detective," he growled, not humored then turned cheerful. "How about lunch tomorrow? I'm at Virtual Play at least half a day updating their computers. We can try that new Thai place a couple of blocks away. I overheard the secretaries say it was pretty good."

"I'll give you a call around noon," she replied. "I have a 'special' assignment in the morning, and I don't know how long that will take."

"Special assignment?" he questioned then appeared enthusiastic. "That sounds important. I guess that means they're finally accepting you for the skilled detective you are."

"I'm not sure I'd go that far," she muttered. "There's a lot of jealousy that someone my age, perhaps even my gender, was promoted above some of the veteran officers."

"You wanted to be a police detective ever since you were a little girl," he remarked. "You've always been an overachiever. You wanted that promotion, and you worked hard to get where you are. Don't let anyone tell you differently."

"Tell that to some of the older officers," she remarked and sighed with defeat. "I know they have their doubts about my abilities because of my age and being a woman."

"Miller respects you, right?"

She considered the question, uncertain how to answer. "Miller's hard to read," she replied. "He's been my partner now for nine months, and I still have no idea how he feels about me being his partner. I know he grumbled about it when he first found out he'd be working with a woman. He's not really much of a talker." She straightened and eyed Rafael. "Enough about my job," she remarked. "How are things going with you at Virtual Play? Have you made any friends at all?"

He shrugged and appeared unwilling to talk about it. "I think the receptionist likes me."

"Dani something or another?" Jade announced with enthusiasm and turned toward him on the sofa, practically giddy at the thought. "She's hot. Are you going to ask her out?"

"Don't get ahead of yourself," he remarked firmly. "She just brought me coffee. We're not picking out china just yet. Although I've heard she has a pet name for me."

Jade stared at him as her enthusiasm faded. "Why do I get the feeling that isn't a good thing?"

"Perhaps because you focus too much on the negative," he casually replied.

"I don't think I'm the problem here," Jade remarked. "We really need to work on your social life." She frowned and sipped her wine.

Chapter Nineteen

Cody Riley's mansion was barely visible from the front gate, which by design. A tall, stone wall surrounded the entire estate meant to keep trespassers out. Large trees, as well as massive shrubs, kept prying eyes from seeing anything that went on even if someone had managed to climb the fence for a look. It was a little after eight o'clock in the morning. The brand new, expensive black Bentley passed through the electronic gates and drove down the road. The heavily tinted windows didn't allow identification of the driver, but Vahn was one of the first guesses. An unmarked police car pulled away from the curb and followed the black Bentley from a safe distance.

The Bentley drove only a few miles down the road to the outskirts of the city and pulled up to a newspaper stand. Vahn got out of the car, purchased a newspaper, and returned to the driver's seat in no particular hurry. The unmarked police car parked nearly half a block away. Jade sat behind the wheel and watched the Bentley pull back into traffic. She put her car into gear and continued to follow from a distance. Only another mile down the road, the expensive car pulled up to a popular coffee shop. Vahn again got out and entered the cafe. The unmarked police car pulled up to the curb and waited. A few minutes later, Vahn returned with his coffee and a paper bag, undoubtedly containing a bagel or pastries. He jumped back into the car and continued on his journey. Jade continued her tail. The Bentley then pulled into the nearly empty parking lot of the Central City Park. The place was usually peaceful until late morning. Jade knew hoping for some drug deal or blackmail scheme was asking too much.

Vahn got out of the car carrying his newspaper, coffee, and the paper bag. He sat on a bench and read the paper while enjoying his coffee and pastry. By his comfy look, he intended to be there a while. Jade sat behind the wheel of her unmarked police car, where she parked within viewing distance of the happily slacking man. She groaned and allowed her head to fall against the seat. Vahn spent an hour in the park just relaxing with his morning paper, obviously in no particular hurry, then finally returned to the car and drove away. Jade again followed him, although by this point she was bored out of her mind. Within a few minutes, the Bentley pulled up to an adult store. She watched as Vahn got out and entered the establishment. Jade pulled up to the curb several cars away and watched the adult store with a bored look on her face.

"What a charmed life this guy leads," she muttered.

An hour had passed as Jade continued to watch the front door of the adult store with complete boredom. She looked at her watch several times then rolled her eyes and groaned. She wondered how many times one man could masturbate while watching porn movies in private rooms. Vahn finally appeared from the adult store with a paper bag and walked along the sidewalk. She found it unusual that he had a paper bag with him. Was it a payoff? She somehow doubted he actually bought something in the adult store. As he approached, Jade sank in the seat and avoided directing attention to herself. Her car door then opened, surprising her as Vahn hopped inside. She debated reaching for her gun, but she knew she'd probably shoot him just for fun. Jade eyed him as he returned the look and smiled.

"While tailing a suspect, isn't it police procedure to follow him inside an establishment?" he questioned. "I could have slipped out the back."

"I wasn't tailing you," she remarked with little interest. "I don't know what you're talking about. Besides, you're parked at a one-hour meter. You wouldn't risk having your boss's very expensive car towed."

"Sexy and smart," he announced with a chuckle. "I'm beginning to think maybe you didn't sleep your way to the position of detective after all."

"Thanks for the vote of confidence."

"As long as you're following me anyway, I think we should have lunch at that new Thai restaurant near the courthouse," he informed her. "I hear the food is excellent."

"You're very convincing," she remarked then allowed her thoughts to stray. She was sure that was the same place Rafael wanted to have lunch.

"So we're on for lunch?"

"No, I wasn't' talking about lunch," she remarked. "I mean you certainly don't act like a hitman."

He laughed at the comment and remained playful. "Probably because I'm not."

"You're more suited to do infomercials."

"That felt like an insult," he remarked while playfully pouting. "Will you be joining me for lunch or should I get it to go and eat in the car with you?" He raised his brows and grinned. "It seems to me we'll be having lunch together either way, so you may as well join me."

Jade studied him a moment, rolled her eyes, and removed her cell phone. She pressed a button and waited.

"Miller, it's me. How much longer?" Jade announced in a bored tone. She waited for a response then groaned at what she didn't want to hear. "No, there's no problem. I'm just dreading this assignment." She again awaited a response. "Yeah, okay. I understand." Jade disconnected the call and pressed another button, only waiting a moment for a response. "Hey, it's me." She listened to the man on the other end. "No, I can't do lunch today. I'm still babysitting Al Capone." Rafael spoke from the other end. She nodded even though he couldn't see it. "Yeah, I'll be home for dinner around six. See you then."

Jade disconnected the call and glared at Vahn.

He smiled and appeared humored. "Al Capone?" he teased. "I'm flattered."

"Yeah, you would be."

"I'll try not to lose you," he announced cheerfully. "It's just a few blocks from here." Vahn got out of the car, leaving the paper bag on the seat.

"You forgot your bag," she informed him.

"No, that's a gift for you."

Vahn closed the door and headed for the Bentley. Jade eyed the paper bag, hesitated, and then opened it with uncertainty. She rolled her eyes and removed the penis-shaped vibrator. She dropped it back into the bag while groaning with disgust.

"This day couldn't possibly get any weirder," she muttered then pulled out behind the Bentley.

Chapter Twenty

Jade entered the elegant Thai restaurant and looked around while marveling at its expensive decor. The restaurant had only recently opened, and despite its price, everyone raved about it. Vahn immediately joined her, having waited inside. She wasn't sure where he'd been hiding when she first entered, but she knew he was enjoying messing with her ability to tail him. He grinned proudly and escorted her to the hostess stand. She eyed him several times while they waited and silently observed his behavior. He seemed like any other man. It was almost a shame he wasted his life working for a low-life scumbag like Cody.

Vahn slipped the young hostess a twenty-dollar bill. "Your most romantic booth."

The attractive hostess smiled knowingly and indicated for them to follow her. Jade glared her disapproval at Vahn, but he easily ignored her look and maintained his smile. Jade followed the hostess to a small, circular booth near the back in a lesser traveled, dimly lit corner. Vahn walked alongside Jade with his hand against the small of her back in a romantic gesture. She casually removed his hand then slid into the booth. If her actions offended him, he didn't show it. Vahn slid in next to her, putting little space between them. She slid a few feet away from him. He again slid in against her.

She cast a glare at him that meant business. "Seriously, you're going to get hurt."

Vahn slid a foot away from her, giving her some space. The hostess handed them each a menu and walked away. He looked around then eyed Jade and smiled.

"Very romantic."

"Not from where I'm sitting," she countered while looking at the menu.

Vahn casually picked up his menu and looked over it. "I've had better first dates."

"This isn't a date," she immediately corrected.

"I'm counting it. I always wanted to date a lady cop," he announced and maintained his schoolboy innocence. "I'm not sure if it's the badge, the gun, or the handcuffs that turn me on most."

"Cops don't date hitmen."

"I'm not a hitman, and I'm not a transporter," he reconfirmed while casting a sharp glare at her. "Ballistics showed my weapon hadn't been fired. I didn't kill that man or anyone else for that matter. We both know that, so stop pretending you have anything on me."

"What were you doing in that parking garage?" she questioned while eying him.

"Can you not be a cop for five minutes and try to enjoy my company?" he practically demanded.

"Why would I want to do that?"

"I don't know--because I was nice enough to let you follow me around all morning so you'd look good for your superiors," he replied.

"You *let* me follow you?"

He chuckled softly. "I spotted you as soon as I left the mansion."

"Yes, and you were meant to," she remarked and returned her attention to the menu.

"Excuse me?"

She set her menu down and focused her attention on him. "Of course Riley would assume we'd follow you, so he'd naturally send you out on some wild goose chase," Jade informed him. "That's why my partner is following the other guy. I'm low on seniority, so I got stuck babysitting you."

He stared at her with some surprise. Rather than call her bluff, he realized she was probably telling the truth and took offense. "That's deceptive and not very ladylike."

"I'm not a lady; I'm a detective."

"Well, I hope you know it's officially over between us," he scoffed.

Jade stared at his serious look but saw the glint of humor beyond his eyes. She couldn't help but smile and laugh. Vahn hid his smile and looked back at the menu.

"I'm starved," he remarked. "Can we order now?"

Chapter Twenty-one

Miller's unmarked police car followed Cody's limousine to Club Zen. The nightclub was located in a decent part of town not far from the business district and within walking distance to many restaurants. The two-story building had recently been converted into the swank club, leaving the second floor gutted until the owner could decide what to do with it. Considering the owner was Cody Riley, there was no telling what sort of shady operation he'd convert the second floor into. It was early afternoon, so the club was closed and without activity. The area surrounding the club was active with those working in nearby buildings heading to and from lunch. Miller pulled alongside the curb just far enough away to avoid being seen but allowing him to see into the alleyway where the limousine parked. He watched the limousine with limited enthusiasm. There was little chance he'd witness anything more than littering from those he'd been following.

A big hulking man, Bernard, got out of the front passenger side and opened the back door to the limousine. Cody stepped out of the limo and buttoned his expensive suit jacket. When Bernard didn't shut the door, Miller assumed there had been another passenger, possibly some cheap tart Cody had picked up at the club. To Miller's surprise, an off-duty police officer in street clothes stepped out of the limousine behind Cody. Miller recognized the seasoned officer as Newman. Newman had a reputation of being at the right place at the right time on numerous occasions throughout his career. The first time Miller crossed his path was eleven years ago when Miller beat him out for the detective position. Newman's career seemed to stall after that, possibly seeing losing the prestigious position to a younger officer as a downfall in his career.

The next time Miller and Newman's paths crossed was during an investigation involving the death of an accountant fleeing from a double homicide at the Strafford Hotel. Newman had been first on the scene and was the only witness to the murder suspect's swan dive off the twelfth-story roof to avoid arrest.

"What the hell is he doing in the company of someone like Cody Riley?" Miller mumbled and kept watch as the three men approached the side door.

There had been another car in the alley. As the three men approached the side door, the man in the parked car got out, also buttoning his expensive jacket. Miller easily recognized the man as Jared Carmichael. Miller shifted in his seat and stared with surprise as Carmichael and his own hired goon approached Cody and his entourage as they headed inside the club through the side door.

"Jared Carmichael," Miller groaned. "The devil himself. Why am I not surprised?"

Once the men went inside, Miller had little choice but to sit and wait within his unmarked patrol car, watching an empty building. He wasn't sitting there long when a small delivery truck pulled into the alley and unloaded cases of alcohol onto a transport dolly. He watched two deliverymen enter the club through the same side door, although only one man seemed to be doing the work. Miller remained suspicious and scribbled the license plate number on his notepad.

Within the empty, nearly silent club, the deliverymen headed through the kitchen and into the main club. They deposited the cases of alcohol near the bar then joined the other men where they passed through a door toward the back of the club. The deliverymen with their transport dolly followed them down the steps into the basement. The basement corridor was tastefully decorated and consisted of two doors on each side. They heard thumping coming from the door on the right, which contained a doorplate indicating it was a closet. There was a men's and lady's restroom on the left, and another door near the end of the hall on the right marked 'employees only'. At the very end of the hall was a steel door resembling a meat locker door. The seven men headed for the meat locker.

Bernard opened the steel door to reveal sides of beef hanging from large hooks. On the floor of the meat locker were black body bags. Cody unzipped one of the bags to reveal a frozen dead man with a look of horror clearly on his face. Cody frowned and shook his head.

"I'll never understand why people think they can cross me and get away with it," Cody remarked then straightened while sighing. He indicated two body bags across the meat locker. "Take those two."

The deliverymen stacked the two black body bags from the opposite end of the locker room onto their dolly then headed out. Cody slapped Newman on the arm and indicated another bag toward the back.

"Check that one," he instructed. "We really should mark these things."

Jared grinned and snorted a laugh from where he stood in the meat locker doorway. Newman headed across the frozen meat locker, crouched alongside the body bag toward the back and unzipped it. He stared at the dead woman, appeared horrified, and sprang to his feet. He spun to face Cody, Jared, and their two henchmen.

"That's my daughter," Newman suddenly cried out while pointing a trembling hand at the dead young woman barely frozen in the body bag.

Cody casually nodded. "Yes," he replied then sighed softly. "I told you not to cross me again, but you didn't listen."

Newman stared at Cody with a look of horror and realization. Bernard removed a gun from his shoulder holster and fired two shots into Newman's chest. He flew backward, tumbled over the body bag, and slid down the wall alongside his dead daughter. Cody patted Bernard on the shoulder and nodded his approval.

"Nice grouping," Cody remarked then indicated the dead cop. "Take care of that."

Both Jared and Cody's henchmen headed across the locker toward the dead man while removing another body bag. Cody and Jared left the locker room.

Cody shook his head. "Good help is so hard to find these days," he remarked with a soft sigh.

"There's always been a huge turnover in employees," Jared informed him. "I'm never surprised when a trusted man turns. Shows you really can't trust anyone, can you?"

They walked along the corridor toward the stairs. "No, I suppose not."

They heard thumping from the nearby closet. Jared indicated the closet. "Anything?"

"Not yet," Cody replied with a bored sigh, "but we're working on it."

Miller sat in his unmarked patrol car watching the building while resting his head against the headrest of the driver's seat. He saw the two deliverymen appear from the side door with two black body bags on their dolly. He sat forward with surprise and watched them load the two bags into the back of the truck. He grabbed his hand radio.

"This is Detective Miller," he announced into the radio. "I need a routine traffic stop on a white delivery van." He watched as the van pulled out of the alley. "Heading north on Whittier Street. License plate Echo Charlie seven nine six four. Suspicious bags in back. Proceed with caution. I repeat; routine traffic stop on a white delivery van."

"Got it," dispatch announced in response.

Miller remained rigid in his seat and continued to watch the building for further activity.

§

A few miles away, a police car with flashing lights had pulled up behind the delivery van. One of the officers waited with the driver toward the front of the vehicle, while the second officer joined the passenger by the back. The deliveryman opened the back door to reveal the two body bags. Blood seeped out from a hole in one of the bags. The officer kept his hand on his holstered weapon and indicated the bag.

"Open it," he ordered.

The deliveryman unzipped the bag to reveal a side of beef thawing. The officer stared with surprise.

"I tried to tell you," the deliveryman announced in a calm tone. "We're taking these to our boss's estate. He's having five hundred guests over for a barbeque at his place. A side of beef and a side of pork."

The officer groaned and shook his head. He removed his hand radio and spoke into it. "We have a negative situation," he announced.

Chapter Twenty-two

Once their meal was served, Vahn and Jade enjoyed their Thai food. The ravings of the secretaries at Virtual Play were correct. She actually felt a little bad that she couldn't enjoy the restaurant with her Uncle Rafael. He enjoyed fine restaurants and usually commented about their cleanliness. Vahn was the king of small talk and also did most of the talking. He'd ask her a few questions, which she refrained from revealing anything personal. When he finally brought up his stint in the military, she was genuinely interested. If his accounts weren't fabricated, his time overseas was well spent while serving his country. He'd seen his share of action and openly admitted losing a few friends along the way.

When he reminisced about his time in the military, she got the sense he missed that lifestyle. For a brief moment, she actually forgot she wasn't at the restaurant on business. He was certainly more interesting and charming than most of her actual dates. She realized how sad that sounded. Was her personal life that dull? When she found herself enjoying their conversation a little too much, she swiftly changed the subject to avoid getting too close. Jade indicated her plate with the chopsticks in her hand.

"This is wonderful," she informed him.

"I was thinking about getting that," Vahn remarked then indicated his food. "This is pretty good too."

"I was wondering how that was," she announced. "I'll have to try that next time."

Vahn picked up some of his food with his chopsticks and held it to Jade's mouth. Jade eyed Vahn with some skepticism then the food he held near her lips.

"It's good. Try it," he insisted.

Jade hesitated then ate the food from his chopsticks. He wasn't wrong. The food was good, although she was just a little untrusting of the man offering it to her.

"Good, huh?" he announced then indicated her shirt. "Oh, you got some on your shirt."

When Jade looked down at her shirt, Vahn snatched some of her food from her plate with his chopsticks. She eyed him as he sampled her meal.

"Hmm. Yeah, that is good."

She stared at him with a strange look. A thousand thoughts raced through her mind as she watched the handsome man sip his wine.

He caught her stare then extended his glass to her. "Did you want some?"

Jade couldn't help but maintain her odd stare even though she didn't want to get involved. "What happened to you?" she finally asked, regretting having said it aloud.

He gave her a strange look. "Excuse me?"

"Someone obviously took time to raise you right," she remarked then shook her head. "Twelve years in the military. Impeccable record. Why did you choose the bad path?"

Vahn stared at her a moment in silence then returned to his lunch and seemed a little less enthusiastic for the subject. "I don't know what you're talking about."

Jade removed her business card and placed it on the table near him. He eyed the card but didn't look at her.

"If you ever decide you want out, I know people who can help," she informed him.

He pushed the card back to her. "I can't have that on me. But I'm good with numbers," Vahn announced. "If I need it, I'll remember it."

Jade placed the card back in her pocket.

Vahn suddenly looked past her and appeared surprised. "Would you look at that?"

Jade looked across the room, curious by what caught his attention. Vahn took more food from her plate with his chopsticks. She glared at him then hid her smile.

"Did you want some more of this?" he asked while indicating his plate.

Jade hesitated then picked at the food on his plate with her own chopsticks while he picked at her plate. After they had finished their meal, the waitress left the bill on the table. Vahn snatched it, placed cash on top of it, and slid out of the booth.

"I can pay for my own lunch," she firmly insisted.

"Yeah, but I ate half of yours."

Jade slid across the booth to the edge of the seat. Before she could stand, Vahn eyed her and motioned to the corner of her mouth.

"You got something--"

She dabbed her mouth where he indicated. Vahn shook his head and reached for her mouth. Without warning, he kissed her quickly on the lips and pulled away just as fast. He flashed a smile and raised his devious brows.

"Told you it was a date," he teased cheerfully. "Later, Detective Wesson."

Vahn left the table without waiting for the punishment he must have assumed would follow from the stolen kiss. Jade remained seated, stared after him with a slightly stunned look, and watched him leave. She shook her head and snorted a soft laugh.

Chapter Twenty-three

It was just after lunch and the programmers had returned to work, leaving everyone busy and the entire floor unusually quiet. Dani typed on her computer, having her usual after lunch conversation with Boyd. Between messages, she got up to stretch her legs and glanced into cubical square to make sure everyone was still alive and awake. It sometimes got too quiet after lunch, and she just assumed they were all asleep at their desks. Not today though. Rafael was back to finish yesterday's updates to the firewalls on everyone's computer. She saw him busily working, leaving the worker from that cubical with nothing to do but gossip with another worker. Dani returned to her desk and checked her message. Her long-winded chat with Boyd was still in progress.

Boyd IM: *"Everything is quiet here. Could fall asleep. How are things there?"*

Dani IM: *"Quiet here too. Can't confirm, but I think those with offices take naps after lunch."*

Boyd IM: *"That's one nice thing about working from home. Can nap and no one knows."*

Dani considered the comment and wondered what that must be like. She could go to work in her pajamas and fuzzy pink slippers, and no one would be wiser. She envisioned Boyd in a pair of silk boxer shorts and bare-chested sitting at his desk on the other end. In her own mind, he looked like one of the hunky men on the cover of a romance novel. She felt her desires suddenly stir then entertained a sexual fantasy involving Boyd and her desktop. She immediately shamed herself, although the ache in her body was very real. Maybe Abby and Janice were right. Maybe it was time she took her relationship with Boyd to the formal introduction level. She found herself desperately wanting to meet him, but that could have had something to do with going without sex for a few months. Before her mind could finish processing the thought as well as the sexual fantasy, her fingers were already typing her desire.

Dani IM: *"Want to get together for coffee?"*

She watched the curser on her screen blink with no response. It wasn't like Boyd to take so long to respond. He was a fast typist and could easily keep up with her in typed conversation. If he stepped away from his computer, he always typed BRB for 'be right back'. She appeared puzzled by the lengthy lag time then became tense as her thoughts raced.

"Oh, God," she muttered. "He's married."

His response finally came through, causing a pang of anticipation within her chest.

Boyd IM: *"This way is better. What if you don't like me? We can never go back."*

Dani IM: *"I already like you."*

Boyd IM: *"Need time to think about meeting. Okay?"*

She felt a terrible pang in her stomach. It suddenly didn't make any sense. Was she wrong about Boyd? Did she actually know nothing about him? Her fingers again typed before her brain.

Dani IM: *"Are you married?"*

As her curser continued to flash, Dani stared at the screen and appeared concerned with each passing second. Did he have to think about it?

Boyd IM: *"No, I'm not married."*

Dani stared at the screen a moment and suddenly became furious. She felt betrayed, and she wasn't even sure why. Her anxiety was rapidly rising, and she needed to step away from the computer before she wrote something she couldn't take back. Dani sprang up from her chair and headed past the cubicles toward the breakroom, needing to cool off. She noted Rafael working busily on his computer and slowed her approach to the breakroom. She couldn't deny she sometimes felt sorry for the strange man since he wasn't very popular among the programmers or their secretaries.

Despite his oddities, he was always nice to her, and she suddenly felt bad for not attempting to know him better. She couldn't admit it to Abby or Janice, but she'd had a particularly disturbing dream last night involving the quirky computer repairman. It was an intense sexual dream that stayed with her all morning, which was possibly the reason she decided it was time to meet Boyd in person. Obviously, her sexual frustrations were manifesting into her dreams, and she needed to meet her needs, or the dreams would continue and possibly increase in erotic nature. Dani paused near the cubicle and smiled at Rafael, although his head was down and he didn't seem to notice her at first.

"I was going to make myself some tea," Dani announced. "Would you like some coffee?"

Rafael realized she was talking to him, lifted his head, and appeared slightly surprised by the offer. "Actually, I wouldn't mind some tea myself."

"Tea it is. Why don't you take a break?" she announced while attempting to sound cheerful despite her foul mood. "I could use the company."

Rafael again stared at her with a slightly baffled look. He was obviously suspicious of the sudden offer of company. He then smiled timidly and nodded. "All right."

§

Rafael followed Dani into the breakroom and suddenly stopped just inside as horror swept over him. The breakroom was a complete disaster. His expression dropped as he stared at the culinary crime scene in disbelief.

"Oh--"

Dani eyed him with a smile while pouring some hot water into two mugs. "What? Something wrong?"

He fidgeted and attempted to remain strong. "Uh, no. Nothing."

Rafael pulled out one of the chairs and eyed it before uncertainly sitting. Dani placed the mug of tea before him and joined him at the table covered with crumbs. Rafael stared at the crumbs and food particles spattered on the table as if he were in a trance.

"You okay?"

"Yes, fine," he mechanically replied then hesitated. "No. No, this is the dirtiest breakroom I've ever set foot in."

"Yeah, some people are slobs," she informed him then casually sipped her tea. "Housekeeping will clean it tonight."

Rafael stared at a blob of mustard on the table. He suddenly jumped up from his chair, ran to the counter, and rummaged through the cupboards. She watched him with surprise.

"Rafael?"

He frantically tore through the cupboards. "I just have to wipe up that mustard."

Several minutes later, Dani held her tea mug while standing alongside Janice and Abby in the breakroom doorway. All three women appeared speechless while watching Rafael scrubbing the kitchen counter like a madman. He'd already tackled the sink and the dirty dishes.

"He's like a demon possessed," Janice gasped.

"Strange *and* creepy," Abby muttered.

"I don't know," Dani remarked while watching him with great interest then seductively ran her finger along the cleavage of her shirt. "For some reason, it's kind of turning me on."

Janice and Abby slowly turned their heads and looked at Dani, who lustfully continued to watch Rafael clean. Janice and Abby looked back at Rafael and appeared to reconsider.

"I wonder if he irons?" Janice questioned.

"The hell with that," Abby cried out. "Does he do toilets?"

Chapter Twenty-four

*L*ater that afternoon, Dani sat at her desk and casually flipped through a magazine while simultaneously ignoring the instant message flashing from Boyd on her screen.

Boyd IM: *"Dani, are you there?"*

Dani ignored the message even though she couldn't quite get into the magazine either. She still wasn't sure what she wanted to do about Boyd, but she wasn't ready to talk to him just yet either. She saw Jade and Miller step out of the elevator into the corridor then enter the lobby through the glass doors. As they approached her desk, Dani quickly straightened, just about ready to jump out of her seat.

"Did you solve the case?"

"Not yet, Miss Phillips," Miller replied as they paused before her desk. "We'd like to have another word with Greg."

"His messages are going to voicemail," she informed them, frowning her annoyance. "I'm not sure if he came back from lunch. I could check his office."

"Mind if we join you?" Jade asked, coming across a lot sweeter than she actually was.

"No, of course not," Dani replied while standing.

Jade and Miller followed her through cubicle square and toward Greg's office halfway toward the back. They entered the office and found Rafael sitting behind the desk working on Greg's computer.

Jade and Dani were moderately surprised to see him there, although Miller was happily clueless. Rafael looked up and saw Jade, Miller, and Dani.

"If you're looking for Greg, he hasn't returned yet," Rafael informed them.

Jade stared at him a moment then raised her brows. "And you are?"

"Rafael Quinn," he replied and flashed a sly grin, playing the game.

"He's our resident computer genius," Dani informed them.

Rafael seemed surprised by the compliment, hid his smile, and then returned to the computer.

Dani fidgeted slightly. "He's upgrading the firewalls after the, uh, *incident*."

Jade shot a look at Rafael and became increasingly interested. "You're in Greg's computer?"

Rafael studied her and leaned forward across the desk as if sizing her up for the first time. "I'm sorry; you are--?"

"I'm Detective Wesson, and this is my partner, Detective Miller," she informed him, continuing the con game as if they'd never met.

Miller gave Jade an odd look then looked back at Rafael with confusion. He refrained from commenting, rolled his eyes while frowning, and looked away with disinterest in their little game.

"Oh, well, in that case, yes," Rafael announced while grinning as he straightened in the chair, "I'm in his computer."

"Anything in there someone *connected* might be interested in?" she asked.

"Connected?" Rafael enquired with a look of surprise. "As in Mafia? To be honest, Detective, I haven't noticed anything beyond game programs."

Miller cast a look across the desk and picked up a matchbook laying on top. It contained the Club Zen logo. Miller showed Dani the matchbook.

"You know this place?"

"Oh, that's the swank club on Fifth," Dani informed him without hesitation.

"Cody Riley's club?" Jade suddenly asked.

"Does Greg frequent that club?" Miller pressed.

"Yes, he goes there almost every Thursday night," Dani casually informed them. "He took me a couple of times--" She hesitated and carefully considered her next comment. "Back when we sort of dated."

Jade walked behind the desk and stood alongside Rafael's chair to take a look at the computer screen. Rafael pretended to be working but instead pressed a button, pulling up a spreadsheet with large monetary amounts on it. Rafael glanced up at Jade as if secretly telling her something. She placed her hand on the back of his chair and nudged his shoulder so no one saw. Rafael clicked on another page. There were more large amounts with account numbers alongside them.

"Kind of strange that he goes to a swank club on Thursdays," Miller remarked. "Most people go to those places when they have off the next day."

"It's pretty crowded on Thursdays," Dani informed him. "There's never any parking. He usually gets there by six. You know, for parking."

Miller and Jade exchanged looks from across the desk.

Jade eyed Dani suspiciously. "That's early to be at a club. Even for a great parking space."

"There are a lot of people there, even at that early hour," Dani replied.

Miller looked at Jade and cleverly raised his brows. "Feel like dancing tonight?"

She laughed softly while sweeping her eyes over him. "You won't exactly blend, Miller."

"I won't have to," he replied with little emotion. "You're flying solo."

Rafael cast a look at Jade with some concern. He obviously didn't care for what was being suggested but was unable to comment on it.

Chapter Twenty-five

Jade and Miller walked in silence across the parking garage attached to the Virtual Play building. Miller looked at her several times, indicating there was something on his mind, but she wasn't going to fish for information.

"Did you and your uncle have a falling-out?" he finally asked.

"No."

Miller eyed her suspiciously. "So why did he act like he'd never met you?"

"He doesn't like sharing his personal life at the office," she replied then shook her head because it honestly made no sense to her either. "He has this paranoid delusion that nobody at work likes him."

"It's not a paranoid delusion," Rafael announced from somewhere behind them, his voice echoing through the silent parking garage.

Both looked back as Rafael approached them from behind. He had a serious look on his face.

"They *don't* like me," he boldly announced.

"They don't even know you," Jade countered with irritation. "You shut them out. You've done that sort of thing your whole life."

"Maybe I don't want them to know me," he retorted then appeared to consider his comment. "Dani invited me to take a break to have tea with her, and I ended up scrubbing down the entire breakroom." He frowned at his own comment. "I even think I'm creepy and strange."

Jade smiled and linked onto Rafael's arm as they walked. "You are creepy and strange, but that's what I love about you."

"That's because you're weird and scary," Rafael muttered in response.

Miller glared at the two then rolled his eyes and shook his head. "You two are perfect for each other," he announced. "A couple of loony tunes."

§

It was three o'clock that afternoon and technically only two hours until quitting time, although most would hang around to nearly six o'clock anyway. Dani continued to flip through her magazine while still avoiding conversation with her internet boyfriend, Boyd. He'd given up for a while, but when she glanced at the computer screen, he'd returned for another attempt to get her to talk.

Boyd IM: *"Didn't mean to upset you. Please forgive me."*

She eyed the screen a moment longer then considered what she had been so mad about in the first place. She hated avoiding Boyd. Their conversations were the only thing she enjoyed in her boring life at the moment. She missed the connection, but she was still bothered by his reaction regarding meeting her. She reluctantly typed a response and hated herself for it.

Dani IM: *"I forgive you."*

Larson entered the lobby and approached the desk while Dani quickly logged off. She straightened in her chair and looked at him, noting the stern expression on his face.

"Good afternoon, sir."

"Good afternoon, Dani," he replied, although he didn't seem interested in small talk at the moment. Larson extended a memo to her. "Would you make copies of this and see that everyone gets one?" He stood proudly and surprised her with his next announcement. "Everyone is staying late tonight. I hired a safety specialist to come in and talk to all the employees. It's mandatory, but everyone will get overtime pay as compensation." He then hesitated and considered something else. "Also, we'll need some sandwich trays for tonight. Have you seen Greg?"

"No, sir," she replied. "I haven't seen him since this morning. His cell phone keeps going to voicemail."

"Try his home phone."

Dani nodded then watched Larson leave the lobby through the glass doors and head for the elevator in the corridor across from her. She waited for him to get into the elevator going 'up' before logging back on her computer. At the same time, she picked up the phone and dialed Greg's home phone number. As she typed into the computer, she listened to Greg's home phone ring endlessly. She finished her message to Boyd.

Dani IM: *"Working late tonight."*
Boyd IM: *"????"*
Dani IM: *"Some safety meeting."*
Boyd IM: *"Can't make you stay late without 24-hour notice."*
Dani IM: *"Yeah, but who's going to remind Larson of that?"*
Boyd IM: *"Good point."*

She didn't have any luck with Greg's home phone number either and gave up when his voicemail picked up. When she looked back at her computer, Boyd sent another message.

Boyd IM: *"If you really want to meet, we can get together."*

She couldn't deny she was relieved to hear, or read, him say that. Unfortunately, she'd had a lot thrown at her that needed to be done immediately, and the masses wouldn't be happy about it.

Dani IM: *"I appreciate that. Can discuss more next week. Gotta hand out fliers. Talk to you later."*

Chapter Twenty-six

Despite the early hour, Club Zen was filled with well-dressed men and women drinking and dancing to the loud music in the dim lighting. Jade walked through the club in a short, revealing black dress. She wasn't a fan of dressing trashy or wearing dresses at all, for that matter. High heels were among her most loathed article of clothing, and she never understood why any woman would want to strap her feet to the insane torture devices. With Miller's two-minute warning before sending her undercover at the club, she was lucky she was able to borrow the dress off Lily on such short notice. She cased the club, finding the packed room not to her liking. She gently touched a concealed transmitter in her ear.

"Okay, Miller," she announced, hoping he'd hear her over the loud music. "I'm here."

"Reading you loud and clear," came his response through the ear transmitter. "Damn that music is loud. How does your generation tolerate that noise?"

"Don't ask me," she remarked. "I'm an enigma in my own generation."

"I'm parked out front," Miller informed her. "Keep me posted."

Jade headed toward the bar while looking around. A large bouncer stood near a door in the back, which she witnessed several people passing through in the short time she'd been in the club.

There was obviously something else happening beyond that door that only a select few were allowed to partake.

"There's a door to the back with a guard and lots of traffic," she informed Miller.

"Any familiar faces?"

"No. None."

Cody Riley walked through the club with his muscular counterpart, Bernard. Cody dressed the part of a wealthy businessman, but everyone knew he was in some way involved with the mob. How involved was the question. Jade had seen pictures of the notorious man, but this was the first time she'd seen him live and in person.

"I see Cody Riley and one of his goons," she announced while attempting to hide that she was talking to herself.

"Tall Neanderthal type?" he responded over her ear transmitter.

"Yeah, that's the one."

"That's Bernard," Miller informed her. "Be careful. He's all muscle and no brain. He'll crush you like a toothpick."

"Considering neither of them has ever seen me before, I should be okay," she replied then drew a deep breath and sighed. "Time to make a few friends."

"Shouldn't be too difficult in that dress," Miller teased over her ear transmitter.

She groaned softly. "Female friends," Jade remarked. "I'm here to socialize not hookup."

"You're right," he replied. "I can't imagine you hooking up anyway."

"How about some radio silence?" she muttered.

"Just shout if you need me," Miller replied over her ear transmitter. "I'll be napping in my car."

Jade shook her head, happy the man in her ear wouldn't comment in her ear all night. She approached a small group of young women close to her age who dressed similarly wearing sexy, revealing dresses. She'd be able to blend better with a group of women her own age, and it would look less suspicious. Unfortunately, Jade wasn't part of that crowd and had nothing in common with that type of woman. She had to hope they were similar to her friend, Lily, and it would be enough to get her through the evening. While Jade made some new friends, Cody leaned against the bar and watched her with more than a passing interest. He nudged Bernard and indicated Jade with a slight nod.

"See that brunette in the black dress?" Cody announced while keeping his eyes glued on Jade.

"I see a dozen brunettes in black dresses," Bernard remarked while scanning the dimly lit room. "Can you be a little more specific?"

"Standing with the three little skanklets," he muttered while frowning.

Bernard again scanned the room and saw Jade with the three regular women. "Yeah, what about her?"

Cody grinned while taking in an eyeful of the young, attractive detective. "She's a breath of fresh air in this place," he announced. "Arrange for an introduction. I'd like to get to know that one a little better. She looks as if she has a brain in her head, despite the company she's keeping."

"Why would you want a smart woman when you can have your pick of clueless ones?" Bernard asked and leaned against the bar alongside him. "Smart ones are a lot of work."

"As if you'd know," Cody muttered and sipped his drink. "I want a woman who can challenge my intellect. Too much eye candy and I can almost feel my brain rotting in my skull."

"Suit yourself," Bernard replied with a dreary sigh. He was about to cross the room when Jared approached and stopped the hulking man.

"Hold off on that hookup," Jared remarked then glared at Cody and gave a slight nod in Jade's direction. "Cody, I'd like you to meet Detective Jade Wesson, homicide division."

Cody suddenly straightened and looked from Jade to Jared. He turned toward the bar and avoided looking at the attractive woman. Jared joined him at the bar and only briefly glanced at Jade, so she wouldn't notice the attention she was drawing.

"No wonder Vahn was tightlipped about his interrogation," Cody muttered. "I'll bet he had a field day with that. What do you want to do about her?"

"Nothing," Jared announced casually and turned toward the bar. "She's not going to find anything we don't want her to find. Just keep an eye on her."

"Two minutes ago, I would have been thrilled to do that," Cody remarked and frowned. "There should be a law against hot women working law enforcement." He then sank into thought. "Detective Wesson. Wesson? Why does that sound so familiar?"

Jared grinned and slapped Cody on the back. "Probably because you killed her parents ten years ago."

He suddenly eyed Jared, who just laughed and walked away. Cody glanced across the club and took in another eyeful of Jade.

"Not exactly a great icebreaker," Cody muttered and shook his head. "So much for my plans for a romantic evening."

Chapter Twenty-seven

Within an hour, Jade and the three women danced together while several men joined them. One man kept pulling Jade against him and attempted to feel her buttocks while they danced. She pushed him away several times while trying to keep from making a scene. She actually wanted to punch the man, but that wouldn't bode well for her cover story. He still didn't take the hint and grabbed her around the waist while dancing with her. She attempted to break free without causing a scene, but he wasn't making it easy for her. The man suddenly released her and took a step back. Jade looked behind her to see what stopped the man in his tracks. Vahn stood behind her glaring at the horny young man.

"Do we have a problem?" Vahn demanded.

"No, Vahn, no problem," the man announced and immediately looked for alternate company.

Miller practically shouted over her ear transmitter, nearly shattering Jade's eardrum. "Vahn's there?" he cried out. "You've been made. Proceed carefully."

Jade casually turned to face Vahn, who glanced over her attire and smiled his approval.

"You clean up nice, Detective," Vahn announced, pleased with what he saw. "Or should we go with Jade?"

"Under the circumstances, we should go with Jade," she casually replied.

Vahn smiled and extended his hand to her, indicating he wanted to dance with her. She uncertainly accepted his hand and allowed him to pull her against him, despite the fast song. He danced close and seductively with her to the pounding club music. Jade was actually surprised he was a good dancer.

"What brings you here tonight?" he asked while keeping his eyes locked on hers.

"I was hoping to run into Greg," she informed him and found it odd that his eyes didn't stray to her exposed cleavage. With his sexually playful mood, she was almost certain he'd be a complete pervert in this situation. "I was told he comes here a lot on Thursday nights."

"I'm afraid I don't know him," he replied then tilted his head. "Boyfriend?"

"The guy comes here every Thursday, and you expect me to believe you don't know him?" she countered with a sly look.

"Lots of people frequent this place," he informed her. "I may recognize a face, but I don't know most of their names. Unless, of course, they're troublemakers."

Finally true to character, Vahn allowed his eyes to stray up and down her then met her gaze with an approving smile while holding her against his body.

"You really look hot."

"You never give up, do you?" she remarked.

"Not when I want something."

"Yeah, me either, but I'm pretty sure we're not talking about the same thing," she teased.

He laughed at the comment. "Let me buy you a drink and see what common ground we can find."

"Unfortunately, you've never told me one thing that was true, so common ground would be very hard to find," she informed him while raising a brow.

"Come on, let me buy you a drink," he pleaded while grinning. "I'll even be nice and let you sit on my lap."

"How generous of you," she scoffed. "Thanks, but I already have a drink. The girls bought me one." She indicated the group of three girls she'd been dancing with earlier.

He eyed the women she indicated then met her gaze. "Those girls?" Vahn suddenly questioned then frowned. "They're bad news. Trust me. They'll get you into trouble before you even know what happened."

Jade laughed and stared into his dark eyes. "*They're* bad news?" she asked. "If they're bad news, what are you?"

"Misunderstood," he replied without hesitation then offered a charming grin.

Jade stared into his eyes while he smiled charmingly. She offered a warm smile, laughed, and patted his face. "Yes, I'm sure you're misunderstood."

Vahn gently took her hand from his face and warmly kissed the back of it as the song faded and immediately went into another. Jade studied him and maintained her smile. She couldn't deny the kiss sent a warm sensation throughout her body, and it bothered her. She knew what he was, and she wasn't about to let his handsome good looks charm her. At the same time, she needed to play her cover story carefully. Drawing him into her circle would almost certainly throw him off. Keep your enemies close.

"Care to join us?" she asked.

Vahn smiled warmly and allowed her to guide him back to their table. The women were surprised to see Vahn as he joined them. Their disapproval was evident, and it made them uncomfortable. Two of the men from the floor joined them as well, filling their table. The men also eyed Vahn with moderate suspicion. He obviously wasn't well liked in certain circles. Jade could understand their feelings. She glanced at the drinks on the table. They all looked alike, and none seemed to be where they were originally left.

"Which is my drink?" she asked.

One of the women pushed a glass in front of her. "Who knows," she replied. "They're all the same anyway."

Jade sipped her drink as the women giggled and goofed around with the two men who'd joined them at the crowded table. As Jade sipped her drink, one of the other men leaned in closer to her and placed his arm around her, since they were extremely crowded at the small table.

Vahn glared at the man on the other side of Jade. "You want to lose that arm?"

The man eyed Vahn's serious look, removed his arm, and turned toward the other girl. He wasted little time placing his arm around her and even putting his hand on her leg. Jade eyed Vahn and attempted to hide her humor at what just happened. She didn't want to encourage him, although he did save her from breaking character and harming the man alongside her.

"Aren't we territorial?" she remarked.

"Yes, we are."

The three women and the two men returned to the dance floor leaving Jade alone with Vahn. Vahn immediately moved in closer to her.

"Finally alone--" He placed his hand on Jade's thigh just below the dress and gently caressed her leg. "You can't deny the sexual tension between us."

Jade eyed his hand then met his gaze. She would have thought her expression would have been enough of a hint for him, but he didn't take the hint.

"I'm thinking you and me; two weeks in Aruba."

Jade was about to come at him with a witty remark when she felt the room breathing. Something was wrong. She again looked at his hand on her leg then back at his lustful grin. She wanted to remove his hand, but she couldn't follow through. Despite her strange feeling, Jade shot up from her chair and immediately regretted the action. She caught his shoulder to keep from falling back down and weighed heavily on him. Vahn stared at her with a curious look that immediately turned to concern. She couldn't be sure if his look was genuine or fake.

"Did you drug me?" she suddenly gasped, knowing Miller would hear her.

She heard Miller shouting through her ear transmitter. "Hold on, Jade. I'm on my way!"

"Of course not," Vahn announced with surprise then stood and attempted to steady her. "I warned you about those girls."

She pulled away from him and immediately clutched her head while the room spun around her. Vahn placed his arm around her waist and helped hold her up. She wanted to push him away but was forced to cling to him to keep from falling. She knew she had to run from him, but she was positive she wouldn't make it a step on her own.

"It's okay. I've got you," he announced firmly. "Try to stay awake. My car is right outside."

Jade could no longer focus on him.

"We need to get you out of here," Vahn announced without hesitation.

Miller hurried into the club through the main entrance and looked around. The large bouncer at the door immediately jumped on him and pulled him back toward the door. Miller protested and attempted to reach for his badge. The guard punched him in the stomach and dragged him out the door. Vahn guided Jade across the club toward the bar and the back door. She clung to him while barely able to support her own weight, and he was soon holding her up.

"Come on, Jade," he announced firmly. "Stay awake. Just a little further."

The entire club suddenly rattled and rumbled. The music skipped, and the lights flickered, nearly going out. Everyone stopped and looked around. The entire building vibrated and shook. People screamed in fear of what was happening. Objects fell from the walls, and chunks of ceiling began to fall. Bottles of booze flew off the shelves, crashing down on the bartenders, who shielded themselves. People screamed and ran for the doors, pushing and shoving their way toward the main entrance. Vahn grabbed Jade and took her down to the floor, seeking shelter beneath one of the tables, and covered her with his body. People continued to scream and shove just before the exit, clogging their only escape. Half the ceiling suddenly collapsed and fell on the large crowd just before the door, their screams immediately silenced. Others heading toward the entrance witnessed the collapse and screamed just before the lights went out.

Chapter Twenty-eight

Dani sat behind her desk at Virtual Play just moments after the meeting finally ended and typed on her computer. It was nearly eight o'clock that evening, and she was exhausted from the long meeting and nearly twelve hours at the office. Somehow, a sandwich platter didn't make up for the late hour spent at work.

Dani IM: *"Meeting just ended. Leaving soon."*

Boyd IM: *"Just felt something--"*

His message puzzled her for only a second before the entire building trembled. Dani clutched her desk and looked around with surprise to the odd vibration.

"What the hell--?"

The entire building suddenly shook violently, frightening her. The lights flickered, objects rattled before crashing to the floor, and the glass on the outer windows suddenly shattered. Everyone within cubicle square screamed. Dani dived beneath her desk with her back to the closed end and clutched her knees to her chest. Drop ceiling and fixtures fell on her chair. Within cubicle square, computers bounced off desks, large cartoon characters plummeted to the floor, and ceiling tile fell, covering everyone with particles as they scattered in an attempt to dive beneath something solid. Several employees dove into the office doorways and braced themselves while others ran out the lobby door to the nearby stairwell. Dani saw people running past her desk where she hid. She was astonished to see them attempting to flee the rumbling building. Being they lived on the east coast, she'd never witnessed an earthquake firsthand, but she didn't think her co-workers should be running around during one.

§

Several employees ran through the nearly vacant parking garage. The entire complex bounced causing them to scream as the massive concrete floor swayed beneath their feet. The cars rose and fell with the floor that somehow offered little to no support anymore. Support beams cracked and buckled from the weight of the shifting. The scattering employees attempted to hold onto cars to keep from falling on the floor now turned into a trampoline of concrete. The top level of the parking garage suddenly collapsed on top of them. With a mighty roar, each level collapsed on top of the other in a domino effect until they hit the bottom in a massive pile of concrete, mangled cars, and a cloud of debris.

§

The entire city shook and rumbled with a deafening roar. Signs fell, roads buckled, bridges collapsed, and parked cars fell into newly opened fissures. Cars driving on the streets during the quake slammed into one another to avoid monster pits within the streets. The unfortunate ones landed within the fissures. Larger buildings swayed and the outer walls cracked while smaller buildings appeared to implode, leaving behind clouds of dust and debris. People on the streets screamed and ran for shelter as they were tossed around by the moving streets. There was mass chaos and confusion as they ran in every direction since there didn't appear to be any safe place for them to seek shelter.

Within Virtual Play, the shaking finally subsided, and the building became still. Dani remained huddled beneath her desk and stared at the debris on her chair and the floor surrounding her desk. She managed to remain unscathed from the traumatic ordeal since her desk was about as solid as they came and offered the perfect shelter. She stared blankly a moment at the mess behind her desk then uncertainly crawled out and looked around the lobby while remaining on all fours. Her computer was covered in debris but, surprisingly, it was still working. She stared at her functioning computer monitor and saw Boyd's urgent message continuing to flash, practically screaming at her.

Boyd IM: *"Dani?"*

Her name was repeated dozens of times; suggesting Boyd was frightened for her welfare. Dani pulled herself up onto her knees and kneeled before her computer, afraid to stand. She grabbed the keyboard and typed her response.

Dani IM: *"Are you okay? Was that an earthquake?"*

Boyd IM: *"I think it was. Stay put. Aftershocks could hit anytime and could be almost as severe."*

Dani IM: *"Checking on others. Be back."*

Dani slowly stood, feeling unsteady on her feet, and made her way through the debris from the ceiling and other fallen objects. She rounded the wall behind her desk and entered cubicle square. To her horror, several cubicles had collapsed. Thankfully, the panels weren't heavy, so they didn't injure those unfortunate enough to be beneath them at the time. Employees moved out from under fallen cubicle panels and other ceiling debris covering them. Some had sustained injuries from falling equipment and oversized cartoon icons, but the injuries she saw were mostly minor cuts and scrapes.

Janice clutched her bleeding arm beneath her torn blouse and looked around. "Abby?" she cried out.

Dani made her way through the debris and hurried to join her friend while scanning the area for Abby. Although it was difficult to see much, she wasn't anywhere to be found.

"Where was she last?" Dani gasped.

"She was right next to me," Janice sobbed with disorientation. "I saw her right before the ceiling panels fell."

"Maybe she took shelter in the office," Dani suggested and hurried to the nearby office door.

Dani opened the office door and suddenly gasped, clinging to the doorknob. Janice ran to join her and clutched the doorframe, sharing the same expression. The collapsed parking garage had taken out part of the office and some of the building. Janice and Dani stood in what remained of the office and eyed the floors above and below them.

"Oh, my God," Dani gasped.

Chapter Twenty-nine

Nineteen remaining employees milled about the debris in the office and searched for unaccounted co-workers, including Abby. Fortunately, they were only finding minor injuries despite all the destruction. They heard a muffled cry from one of the overturned filing cabinets. Larson and Peterson pulled a large filing cabinet away from one of the desks to reveal Abby curled beneath the desk in a tiny ball. Janice and Dani helped her out and pulled her to her feet. She remained unsteady and disoriented, although mostly unscathed except for a few scratches and bruises. She hugged her friends then immediately pulled away and stared at them with shock.

"What the hell? And I mean what the hell?" Abby cried out. "Was that an earthquake?"

"We're on the east coast," Janice reminded them while placing a trembling hand to her bruised temple. "Is that even possible? Maybe a plane crashed, or a bomb exploded."

Brad approached with his cell phone in his hand. "The cell towers are still working and so is the internet," he informed them. "They're saying it was definitely an earthquake."

Peterson stood in the office doorway overlooking the collapsed parking garage and stared at the mostly dark city. Some buildings had power while others didn't, and it seemed as if every streetlight was out. They could see several collapsed buildings and other signs of visible damage from their elevated view on the ninth floor.

"The whole city is fucked up," Peterson informed them while briefly glancing back.

"I can't believe we still have power," Janice remarked and nervously looked at the ceiling.

Several light fixtures dangled down, hanging by their power cords.

Brad consulted his cell phone and shook his head in disbelief. "They're asking that everyone at a secure location remain there," he announced then looked at his co-workers. "There are concerns about aftershocks, fires, and mass chaos on the streets for emergency crews." He ran his fingers through his hair. "We're officially in a state of emergency."

Larson straightened proudly and immediately took charge of the situation, his commanding presence catching everyone's attention. "I realize the parking garage is gone, and everyone is concerned, but this building is secure," he informed them. "It's important that we stay here and remain calm."

People began to chatter about loved ones, tossing calm out the window.

"I know you're concerned about your family and friends," Larson announced firm and loud, silencing everyone, "but you won't do them any good getting yourselves killed trying to reach them. I'll have security lock the doors. This building is safe."

"Lock the doors?" Janice gasped.

"Chaos on the streets," Brad reminded her while raising a brow. "Some of that will be looters."

Janice appeared horrified, clutched her chest, and withheld her gasp. "Oh, God!"

"There's a first aid kit in the breakroom," Dani announced while attempting to sound calm for the sake of the others. "We should take care of those with injuries."

"I'll take roll call and make sure we're all here," Abby announced and scrambled to find a pen and paper.

"I saw a few people run out of the office," Janice gasped with horror.

"Well, I hope they didn't go to the parking garage," Peterson muttered.

The employees exchanged concerned looks because they were almost certain that's where they would have headed.

"I'll check the stairway," Dani remarked while choking on her words.

"I'd better go with you," Brad announced and hurried to join her, his concern showing. "I think we should stick together on account of aftershocks."

"Excellent idea," Larson announced and swept a look over those remaining in the cluttered cubicle square. "No one travel anywhere alone."

Chapter Thirty

Dust and debris filled the dimly lit nightclub while electricity crackled from an exposed wire somewhere in the demolished ceiling. A large support beam had fallen partially to the floor from above, revealing a large chunk now laying on the floor. People could be heard coughing, moaning, and crying. Jade slowly opened her eyes and stared at a sideways view of the club from where she lay face down on the floor. It only took her a second to realize she was pinned to the floor as she felt massive pressure on top of her body nearly constricting her breathing. She gasped for air and clawed at the debris on the floor. She was unable to move out from under whatever was on top of her.

Jade cried out softly and made an effort to push out from under the heavy object pinning her. She could hear the table move. She pushed again, getting her hand beneath her, and toppled what was holding her down. She saw Vahn roll off her with her last thrust, casting his motionless body onto the floor. He lay unresponsive on his back, bleeding from the temple while covered in debris. A small part of the ceiling had collapsed on top of the table they'd been huddled beneath. The table and Vahn absorbed most of the impact, protecting her. Jade stared at him a moment as her heart pounded, uncertain if he was even alive, then slid toward him and felt for a pulse. When she discovered he was alive, she weakly pulled herself to her feet, swayed slightly, and stumbled over mounds of debris to the bar.

Between being drugged and having the house fall down upon her, she could barely stand on her own feet. Jade removed a bottle of water and a rag from the bar then hurried back to Vahn. She practically fell to the floor alongside him, still dizzy herself, and cleaned his bleeding temple while leaning over him.

"Vahn, can you hear me?"

Vahn suddenly jerked awake, clutched Jade's hand on his face, and looked around with disorientation. He immediately groaned, shut his eyes, and lay still on the floor.

"What the hell hit me?" he gasped.

"I'm guessing the ceiling."

Vahn opened his eyes and stared at the massive opening to the second floor. "Oh, shit--"

"The table must have absorbed most of the impact," she added while attempting to clear the dust from her throat.

He cringed with pain and groaned. "My back disagrees with you."

Vahn slowly sat up and clutched his bleeding head. Jade helped steady him even though she wasn't exactly steady herself. She took a few swallows of water from the bottle then offered the rest to him. He took several swallows then gave her a quick once over with concern.

"Are you okay?"

"Yeah, I was beneath you," she informed him then offered a tiny smile. "Thank you."

"For what?" he muttered and shut his eyes, enduring the pain in his head. He managed a tiny, humored smile. "I was just looking for an excuse to jump on you."

She ignored the sexual innuendo and studied him. "Are you okay?"

"Other than feeling like a ceiling fell on me, yeah, I'm fine," he remarked then glanced at her. "But we may have to forgo sex tonight."

She groaned and rolled her eyes. "Yeah, you're fine." She attempted to move to her feet. "I'd better check on the other people. I think a lot have been hurt."

Vahn nodded and made an effort to stand but fell back onto his backside. He panted heavily and waved her off.

"I'll catch up with you," he groaned.

§

*C*ody pulled himself from the rubble and looked around the disastrous area that was once Club Zen. He stared in disbelief at the destruction and the collapsed second floor. It only took another minute or two for a quick head count to reveal the horrifying reality of the situation. He ran his fingers through his dust-coated hair and shook his head.

"Jesus," he cursed softly.

The patron total was only about twenty-five percent of what it had been prior to the quake. Bernard staggered toward him while wiping blood from his forehead.

"What the hell happened?" Bernard demanded while looking around. "Was that an earthquake? On the east coast?"

Cody shook his head and continued to scan the room. "It most certainly was," he replied then looked at Bernard. "Have you seen Jared?"

"No, not since the city took a shit," he muttered.

"Find him," he ordered. "Then you need to collect the others and start crowd control. This building isn't secure. We need to get these people out of here before the whole place comes down on our heads."

Bernard nodded then made his way through the rubble. Jared stumbled toward Cody from the back. He was slightly battered with several cuts and bruises.

"Well," Jared announced with a groan. "Now I've seen everything. A massive earthquake on the east coast."

Cody continued to scan the club, still stunned by what he was seeing. "Yeah."

"We need to get our VIP guest and get the hell out of here," Jared informed him. "We can't afford to have first responders show up and find our little operation in the basement. I suggest we purge the place."

Cody looked at Jared with some surprise. "You realize there are probably one hundred people beneath that rubble, right?" he demanded. "We've got bigger problems."

"No, you have bigger problems," Jared snarled. "I don't give a rat's ass about your precious club. I'm not going to jail because you're feeling sentimental about a few dozen drunken party kids. You evacuate anyone with a pulse, and then you purge this dump. I don't want any evidence left that can incriminate me. If you cross me, you'll wish you were beneath that rubble along with them. Understand?"

Cody frowned and nodded. "Yeah, I understand."

Chapter Thirty-one

Nearly thirty people roamed around within the debris of the dimly lit nightclub. Thankfully, most only had minor injuries, but it was disheartening when they realized there had been over two hundred people in the club just before the quake hit. There had been so much chaos when the building shook; no one really knew what had happened. Had some made it outside? Many had been shoving their way to the main exit that was now blocked by a huge chunk of ceiling. As they searched beneath tables and broken chairs, they found several people dead in the rubble. The number of those found dead or alive was still just a fragment of how many patrons had been in the building.

A few patrons attempted to open the rear exit to the alley between the club and the professional building next door. Despite their combined efforts, the door wouldn't budge. Others worked tirelessly to remove chunks of the second floor from the main entrance. It was within the massive amount of rubble they found dozens of dead bodies with countless more possibly beneath the larger portions of ceiling they couldn't move. Maybe some had made it outside, but it was obvious that most hadn't.

Sirens were heard in the distance, but none was heard directly outside the club. They didn't seem to be getting any closer, leaving those trapped within the partially collapsed building concerned about a possible rescue. Vahn fiddled with his cell phone, but no one was able to complete their calls. They kept hearing 'all circuits are busy' with an irritating tone. Jade approached Vahn as he made several attempts to get a call through.

"Anything?" she asked.

"The cell towers are working, but they're overloaded," he informed her. "I texted a message to a few people, but I haven't gotten any responses yet."

"Judging by the amount of damage here and the sounds of sirens in the city, they're not finding us for a while," she informed him. "They'll be responding to fires, car accidents, and collapsed buildings visibly noticeable. I'm guessing this structure appears intact from the outside."

"You can give me the good news anytime," he muttered under his breath.

"I don't have any good news at the moment," she remarked while looking around. "There are two dozen dead people beneath that collapsed ceiling by the main entrance and probably another dozen closer to the doorway." She removed her ear transmitter and looked at it while frowning. "Miller's not answering." She replaced the ear transmitter. "Either the signal is lost along with the phones or something happened to him as well." Jade looked around and rubbed her sore arm. "We can expect powerful aftershocks that could easily bring down the rest of this building. We're not safe in here."

"Something pretty heavy is blocking the back door," Vahn informed her. "Some guys have been working on it, but it's not budging."

"Aren't there any windows in this place?"

"Upstairs," he remarked and indicated the large hole in the ceiling. "There might be small ones in the basement, but I don't really know."

Jade looked at the back door that once contained a bouncer. "Is that the basement?"

"Yeah."

She looked up to the missing ceiling and debated her next move. "How do we get up there?"

He nodded toward a large pile of ceiling. "The stairs are beneath that mound of rubble. The second floor is unstable enough. We shouldn't be up there."

"Then we should try the basement," she suggested. "Maybe there's an unblocked window."

Vahn looked at the basement door then at Jade with little emotion. "I'll check it out," he informed her. "You should wait here."

"I'll fit through tighter spaces than you."

His look was stern. "You need to stay here."

"Seriously?" she launched with irritation while firmly placing her hands on her hips. "You think I'm concerned about your boss's illegal activities at a time like this? I think we all have bigger worries."

The building vibrated harshly, and debris fell from the ceiling pelting them. The ceiling groaned above them. Vahn grabbed Jade, pulled her against him, and took her down to the floor alongside the bar, shielding her with his body. People screamed as the few remaining lights flickered. Jade clung to Vahn, held her breath, and buried her face into his neck. Few things frightened her, but this was one of those moments in her life where she was actually afraid. She had visions of the building collapsing on top of them as it had those unfortunate people by the door. That she sought comfort in Vahn's arms was the most frightening part. Normally, she didn't want to be held; she didn't need to be held. Today was not normal. The rumbling stopped, and she felt Vahn's muscles unclench. He loosened his grip then looked at her as she slowly removed her face from his neck. Their lips nearly touched as she stared into his eyes. She knew he saw her fear, and she wished she could have hidden it better. She tensed while staring at him.

"This is the first time I've ever felt helpless," she announced almost timidly. "I don't like it."

"Trust me; you're not alone."

Vahn kissed her quickly but warmly on the lips, surprising her, then pulled back and smiled, revealing his sincerity, as he brushed the hair from her face.

"I'm going to get you out of here," he gently informed her. "We're going to be just fine."

She stared into his eyes not far from hers and no longer saw Cody's hired goon. She saw the gallant soldier willing to sacrifice his life for hers. The way she stared into his eyes was all the encouragement he needed. He touched her face then leaned closer, lowering his mouth to hers for another kiss. Jade placed her hand to his debris coated shirt and spoke just as his lips were about to touch hers.

"I'm going with you into the basement," she insisted.

Vahn's smile faded into a frown as he pulled away from her. He groaned with disappointment and stood. She immediately straightened as well.

"Don't involve yourself in something that doesn't concern you," he announced sternly, his mood changing. "You have no backup, and I can't protect you."

"If this building collapses, we're all dead," she announced while glaring at him. "We need to find a way out."

"The answer is no, Jade. If I'm caught taking you down there, it's both our asses," he informed her while placing his hands firmly on her bare, slightly scraped shoulders. "You need to stay here and help the others. Protect and serve, remember? I'll let you know the situation when I return."

Vahn released Jade and was about to leave when he suddenly hesitated and appeared to consider something. He placed his hand behind her neck and kissed her quickly but passionately on the mouth. Before she could protest, he broke off the kiss, flashed a smile, and hurried away. He snapped his fingers to one of the bouncers, Bruno, and pointed at Jade.

"Keep an eye on my girl," he announced gruffly to the big man. "Don't let her out of your sight."

Bruno gave a nod and focused his attention on Jade. She glared at Vahn as he headed through the back door then looked back at Bruno.

Chapter Thirty-two

Vahn walked down the basement stairs then stopped a few feet short of the bottom step leading into the corridor. Thigh high water flooded the basement. He stared at the flooded corridor and appeared to contemplate his next move. He ran his fingers through his dirt coated hair then headed down the last few steps into the water.

"Oh, shit--" Jade gasped from behind him.

Vahn turned when he heard her and stared at her with surprise. "How did you get down here?" he demanded. "Bruno was watching you."

"Bruno isn't very bright," she replied then indicated the water. "What happened?"

"I don't know," he groaned and again looked around. "Water main break perhaps?"

Vahn trudged through the water with Jade following him. A dead bouncer floated in the water having suffered a head injury. They heard screams and pounding on the door just a few feet down the corridor. Vahn approached the dead man, removed a set of keys and unlocked the nearby door. Several people pushed their way out of the flooded room in a state of panic. Jade peered inside the room and observed the flooded casino. Tables and chairs floated along with chips, cards, and a dozen or more bodies. A large ceiling mirror was broken and submerged in the water, indicating the dead people were undoubtedly struck by it. At the moment, Jade was more concerned with the death toll than the illegal gambling. When she eyed Vahn, he must have assumed she was assessing the illegal activity and glared back at her in response. She wasn't worried about Cody's little side business right now.

"Come on," he muttered. "Let's go."

As they turned within the flooded corridor to follow the fleeing gamblers, Jade heard a thump within one of the rooms in the corridor not far from the casino. She trudged through the thigh-deep water and attempted to open the nearby closet door. It didn't budge. She knocked on the door and listened for any response. She heard a thump beyond the door. Jade turned to Vahn with concern.

"There's someone in there," she informed him.

Vahn moved past her and unlocked the door with the bouncer's keys, revealing a small closet. Greg was gagged and tied to a chair with the water nearly up to his waist where he sat. Jade trudged through the water into the room and removed his gag. The door closed and locked behind her. She turned and looked at the locked door with surprise.

"Not exactly a brilliant move, Detective," Greg announced while gasping from his ordeal.

Jade removed the duct tape binding his wrists to the arm of the chair. "When a guy saves your life, it makes you forget that you aren't supposed to trust him," she informed him.

Greg reached into the water to untie his ankles then stood within the thigh-high water. He stared at her and appeared surprised by her less than concerned attitude.

"Why aren't you worried?" he asked.

"Because I'm smarter than he is," she remarked and approached the locked door.

"Not from where I'm standing."

"Have a little faith," she announced. "This dress may look a little short and revealing, but I have one or two gizmos up my sleeves."

"Too bad you don't have any sleeves," Greg remarked and casually leaned against the doorframe while watching her.

Jade removed one of her high heels, slid open the bottom, and removed a lockpick from a hidden compartment. She replaced her shoe. "I'm lucky I have a genius uncle who's into gizmos, gadgets, and secret compartments."

Greg stared at the lockpick with surprise then eyed her and laughed softly. "If we get out of this, I'd love to shake your uncle's hand."

Jade worked on manipulating the lock. "Since we have a few minutes, maybe now you'd like to tell me what you wouldn't tell me before."

"I have a bit of a gambling problem," Greg replied while sinking against the wall near her. "I owed Cody Riley a lot of money, so he let me work it off by electronically laundering money for him. A lot of money."

"But then something went wrong?"

"I discovered the casino wasn't all he was into," Greg continued and frowned. "Knowing what I knew was too much, so I started compiling evidence against him, but I needed enough to make him and his entire operation go away or else he'd make me go away. You know what I mean?"

"What stopped his hitman from doing that?"

"I moved his money around as an insurance policy," Greg informed her. He managed a tiny grin. "If they killed me, nearly a billion dollars would die with me--virtually."

"That's a good way to get tortured before being shot in the head," she muttered.

"Yeah, I hadn't really thought that through."

"So why not tell us after the attack?" she asked while casting a quick look at him and continued with the door lock.

"I didn't have enough evidence. I needed a couple of days," he replied then sighed softly. "Time ran out. They grabbed me when I went to the vendor on the corner for a coffee."

"So besides illegal gambling, what's the sorry sack of shit into?" Jade asked.

"The usual," Greg replied with a sigh. "Prostitution, drugs, smuggling."

"What else?" she asked and stopped to eye him. "You wouldn't suddenly feel guilty over that."

Greg frowned and appeared ashamed, almost unable to admit what he knew. "Underage Asian girls," he replied reluctantly. "I was so enraged when I found out, that I just wanted to put a gun to his head and pull the trigger."

Jade returned to picking the lock, although she was letting the new information circulate within her head. "So who offed the hitman?"

"I don't know, but my money is on that Lott guy," Greg replied while suggestively raising his brows. "He gives a lot of orders, and no one questions him. A lot of people around here are afraid of him. He and that Trent guy got into it one night upstairs. I thought he was going to kill him." He watched her work on the lock. "One week later, Trent turns up dead. A little too coincidental, if you ask me."

"He swore he'd never seen Trent before."

"I'm sure he lies about a lot of things," Greg muttered then eyed her. "After all, he did lock us in here."

Jade sprung the lock and replaced the pick to her shoe. Greg quickly straightened and appeared ready to pounce when she opened the door.

Jade stopped him from running out of the closet and stared into his eyes. "Don't be in a hurry," she announced firmly. "We have a situation upstairs."

"What situation? The explosion?"

"It wasn't an explosion. It was an earthquake," she informed him then groaned. "We're trapped. There's no way out just yet, which means we'll need to stay out of sight."

"There's a storage room in the corridor just beyond the basement door," he informed her. "If we can slip through the door at the top of the steps, they'll never see us in that corridor. We can hide in the storage closet."

Jade lifted her dress and removed a small, semiautomatic from a thigh holster. Greg eyed her leg with surprise.

"Then that's where we'll go. You need to stay behind me and keep quiet," she commanded.

Greg nodded. "Yeah, sure," he announced. "I'll stay behind you."

Chapter Thirty-three

Dani cleared the debris off her seat and shook the dust off her computer keyboard. She jumped into her chair behind the receptionist desk, which was cluttered with ceiling debris, and frantically typed on the keyboard. Janice and Abby paced in front of the desk and watched their friend attempting to contact Boyd. Once she finished typing, she could barely sit still while impatiently awaiting a response. When Boyd responded back, she looked at her friends with concern in her eyes.

"Boyd says the streets are filled with panic," she informed them. "A lot of the city has lost power. The police are concerned about looters and criminal mischief."

What Boyd was telling them really wasn't news. They could hear alarms and sirens wailing continuously outside the building. Some were ambulances; some the fire department and a lot were the police. Dani continued to type.

"I'm glad we're locked in here," Janice remarked while insecurely rubbing her shoulders beneath her moderately torn and dirty blouse.

"He said a curfew has been implemented," Dani informed them while watching the screen.

They could hear the faint sounds of gunshots coming from the streets below. All outside sounds were magnified by the broken windows and the missing portion of the building which had once contained the parking garage. Janice and Abby looked around and listened to the sounds from the streets seemingly echoing throughout the city. Gunshots were heard sporadically from that moment forward.

"Do you hear that?" Abby gasped.

"He says there's a lot of shooting going on everywhere," Dani replied while studying her screen and the messages that seemed to fly onto the computer. Boyd was a fast typist, but he was typing a marathon now.

Larson approached her desk, watched a moment, and appeared curious. "Are you talking to someone?"

"Yeah," Dani replied without looking away from her screen, not wanting to miss the rapid-fire messages.

Boyd's messages were almost too fast for her to keep up with them. She'd forgotten how fast he could type when he was passionate about something.

"Dani's boyfriend has access to news," Abby informed Larson. "He's giving us updates on the aftermath of the quake."

The building suddenly rattled and vibrated. Everyone grabbed onto the large desk for support. The tremor only lasted a minute or two before subsiding, but everyone's nerves were already frayed from the initial quake and excessive damage.

"I'm hearing a lot of gunshots," Larson informed them. "The streets must be chaos out there."

Dani suddenly stared at her computer as alarm swept over her. "Oh--"

Janice panicked and rounded the desk, now standing behind Dani's chair while peering over her shoulder. "Oh, what?"

"He just heard that two rival gangs are going at it," Dani replied, unable to look away from the computer screen. She held her breath a moment then eyed her friends and Larson. "The police are calling this side of the city a war zone. He says to keep the building locked and to stay inside."

Larson immediately straightened and sprang into action. "I'd better have Ralph patrol the lobby downstairs," he announced then hurried from the office through the cracked glass doors.

As the women listened, the sound of gunfire seemed to increase. All three held their breath and looked at one another with concern.

§

Jade's cell phone was nestled in the center console of the unmarked police car. It lit up and vibrated, the ID reading 'Rafael'. She had ten missed calls. Undoubtedly all were from Rafael. Club Zen could be seen seemingly unscathed beyond Jade's unmarked police car parked along the curb. To the right side of the two-story nightclub, the building alongside it had collapsed against the outer wall, which explained why the alley door couldn't be opened. Several parked cars were smashed together from the fissures left behind on the streets. Streetlights were down, and an electric pole had fallen across the road itself. The streets were dark and appeared mostly empty in anticipation of aftershocks.

Nearby buildings had smashed windows and security alarms in some of them wailed, although their calls went unanswered. The police had their hands full with escalating crime, injuries, and collapsed buildings. At the moment, the stores in the business district appeared safe from looters, although it was doubtful that would last long. A bruised and bloodied Miller sat in his own unmarked car with the police radio in his hand and his cell phone discarded on the passenger seat. He'd given up on his cell phone and resorted to the police radio, which still worked.

"Officer needs assistance at Club Zen," he announced into the radio. "Exits are blocked by collapse. Undercover inside. Possible situation. Backup desperately needed."

"No available units," dispatch responded, the woman sounding slightly frantic herself. "The entire city has collapsed buildings, impassable roads, and fires. There's a war involving two or more rival gangs. Looting and rioting is everywhere. The National Guard is en route. ETA four hours."

"Four hours?" Miller suddenly shouted into his radio. "This is my partner's life!"

"Sorry, Detective, it's every partner's life tonight," the woman responded in a defeated tone. "We have ten officers down, another fifteen not responding, and the violence has just started to escalate on nearly every street. Officers from just about every nearby city have been called in to assist."

"Yeah, I copy." Miller threw his radio with disgust. He tapped his ear transmitter. "Jade? Jade, do you copy?"

There was complete silence from his ear transmitter. Miller cursed softly and looked at the nightclub across the street from him.

He eyed the second-story window just above the rubble from the collapsed building and appeared to consider something. He groaned at his own idea and nervously scratched his head.

Chapter Thirty-four

Dani continued to type onto the computer, her conversation with Boyd moving as swift as if they were talking face-to-face. She'd never typed so fast in her life, but there were things they both needed to say. Boyd's messages were mostly updates and warnings. Janice and Abby paced in front of her large desk and played with their cell phones in apparent disgust. Cell service was spotty, but overloaded, keeping anyone from getting through to his or her loved ones. Larson hurried into the office through the cracked lobby doors. His expression was concerning.

"Ralph is missing, and the front door is open," he informed them. "Someone got into the building. I locked out the first elevator on the ground floor lobby, in case someone attempts to use it. The second elevator is locked out on our floor, but I need help barricading both sets of stairwell doors."

Janice and Abby hurried past Dani's desk to alert the others. The sound of gunshots could be heard somewhere on one of the lower floors of the building. The employees within what was left of cubicle square panicked after hearing the shots. Four employees ran across the office to the lobby doors.

"No, we need to stay. We need to secure the stairwell door," Larson cried out, attempting to stop them from leaving. "It's not safe out there!"

Dani watched several co-workers scatter out the main door and run down the nearby stairwell. Larson, Peterson, and Brad hurried out the lobby door and attempted to secure the stairwell. Dani felt panic sweeping over her, feeling as if everything was falling apart. She frantically typed on her keyboard.

Dani IM: *"Building compromised. Larson says they're inside. Heard gunshots. Everyone is running scared. What should I do? I'm scared."*

The curser blinked a long moment as Dani squirmed in her chair and nervously looked around. Boyd's message appeared and stunned her.

Boyd IM: *"Stay there! I'm coming for you!"*

Dani stared at the screen and almost gasped in response. She frantically typed while crying out. "No! No! It's too dangerous! Don't die because of me!" She waited, but there was no response.

Dani IM: *"Boyd, please, don't go out!"*

There was still no response.

Dani IM: *"Boyd?"*

Larson, Brad, and Peterson hurried back inside and frantically turned out the lights.

"Everyone find a place to hide," Larson cried out. "We're going to stay quiet and out of sight in the event they get through. No one plays hero."

Larson motioned Dani away from her desk, forcing her to join the others within cubicle square.

*P*eople were looting stores through broken doors and windows as alarms wailed. Buildings burned, cars were piled up, and people ran and screamed in the dimly lit streets. Building alarms were heard from just about every street as police and fire sirens echoed throughout the city. Miller climbed the rubble of the imploded building in an attempt to reach Club Zen's second-story fire escape. Gunshots were heard close by. Miller flattened himself on top of the rubble, hiding himself in the shadows, as he looked at the streets below. Gang members, some mere teenagers, ran through the streets shooting at one another. He watched nearly a dozen or more young men dressed in their finest looting attire with masks covering their faces as they shot at one another.

"This town has really gone to shit," Miller muttered and waited for them to pass through.

Once the gang had moved from his street, Miller continued crawling on the rubble toward the fire escape. He grabbed onto the metal rail and pulled himself onto the landing. It groaned slightly beneath his weight but seemed to hold. Miller rested a moment while panting heavily. He looked down the incline of rubble he'd successfully scaled and seemed amazed at how far he'd actually climbed.

"I'm getting too damned old for this shit."

Chapter Thirty-five

The dozen or more partially soaked people from the basement shivered around the bar with drinks to settle their nerves. The original thirty remaining survivors from the main club level continued to move rubble and dead bodies away from the front entrance. As they got closer to the opening, there were more bodies than actual rubble. Electricity continued to crackle from above in the partial remains of the second floor. Ceiling and debris fell onto the main floor, causing several panicked screams from those fearing the rest of the building would collapse. Cody, Bruno, Vahn, and four other men rushed across the debris-covered room toward a far corner.

Jade and Greg appeared within the basement doorway, made certain the area was clear, and then slipped down the hallway not far from the basement. Jade paused just out of sight and peeked around the corner, watching the seven men in the near distance. They finally broke up their meeting. Bruno, Cody, and two of the other men headed toward the main entrance to assist in digging their way out while Vahn, Bernard, and another man, Les, headed for the basement door. Jade waited until they went down the steps then crept into the basement behind them.

Once she reached the bottom of the steps and the flooded area, she saw the three men removing a duffel bag from a nearby utility room. They headed through the water and into the casino while talking among themselves. Several minutes passed. Jade moved into the water and made her way to a nearby bathroom to seek cover. She entered the bathroom and waited in the thigh-high water alongside the doorway of the darkened room. She peered into the corridor through the partial door opening and could hear the men's voices as they left the casino.

Vahn cast the empty duffel bag aside, allowing it to float in the water, and then cast looks at Bernard and Les. "I'll finish here and bring the geek with me," he announced. "Tell the boss the explosives are in place."

"You have the remote?" Bernard asked.

"Yeah, I have it," Vahn reported.

"You gonna take care of the cop?" Les demanded.

"The explosives will take care of that for me," Vahn replied without emotion.

"Just make sure the club's been evacuated before you push that button," Les reminded.

"I think I can handle it, Les," Vahn muttered with annoyance at the man.

The two men waded through the water down the hall and eventually headed up the stairs. Vahn placed the remote control into his pocket, removed some keys, and hurried through the water for the closet door. He unlocked the door, opened it, and stared into the empty closet with a surprised look.

"Jade?"

As Vahn turned, Jade kicked him in the chest, although her kick lacked momentum from the water. He struck the nearby wall, feeling enough of the kick to make him wince. Jade aimed her gun at his face while glaring at him.

He gently rubbed his chest while staring at her and completely ignoring the gun. "Jesus that hurt!"

"That's referred to as 'unnecessary roughness'," she informed him then sneered, "but I enjoyed it."

"Next time, take off the heels first," he remarked then looked around. "Where's the geek?"

"Someplace safe," she informed him. "Very slowly remove your gun from your shoulder holster with two fingers."

"As much as I'd love to play with you, we don't really have time."

"Fine, we'll do it the easy way," she scoffed while replacing her gun to her thigh holster.

Vahn's head tilted as he watched with interest and possible desire. She suddenly punched him in the face, knocking him back against the wall, and then kicked him in the groin, again losing momentum from the water. The kick was still hard enough that he doubled over. She snatched his gun from his shoulder holster and aimed it at him.

Vahn clutched himself and groaned painfully. "Okay, that was just plain mean."

"Just doing my job," she snarled while glaring a hateful look at him. "Just like you were doing yours when you locked me in that closet."

He slowly straightened while staring at her with surprise. "That wasn't me," he insisted. "Cody did that."

"I've never met your boss," she informed him. "You told him who I was."

"He had you checked out," Vahn assured her. "He didn't need me for that. I came down here to rescue you."

"Bullshit. You came down here to kill me," she lashed out with hostility. "I know who and what you are."

"I thought we were past that," he demanded in an irritated tone. "If I wanted to kill you, I wouldn't have saved you from the ceiling collapse."

Vahn leaned against the wall and gingerly rubbed his face. "You hit like a girl." He then rubbed his chest and groaned. "But you kick like a mule."

"You're going to defuse the bomb, or I'm going to target practice on your body," she announced then aimed the gun at his crotch. "Starting with your favorite body parts."

"What makes you think I know how to disarm it?" he asked and tilted his head. "You don't want the bomb to go boom; you don't press the button. That's as much as I know."

"Give me the remote."

Vahn removed the simple car remote and extended it to her. As she took the remote, Vahn snatched his gun from her hand and aimed it at her. Jade appeared surprised by his reflexes.

"Classic rookie move, Jade," he informed her while grinning. "By the way, that's the remote to my car."

Jade frowned and tossed it over her shoulder.

Vahn motioned with the gun. "Against the wall. Hands where I can see them."

Jade moved past him and placed her hands on the wall near her head. Vahn moved closer to her from behind, ran his hand slowly under her dress along her thigh, and removed the gun from the thigh holster. He placed it in his jacket pocket then returned his own gun to his shoulder holster. He moved against Jade from behind, placed his hands over hers, and held them to the wall in a seductive position. Jade remained still and appeared to consider her next move. While pressed against her from behind, Vahn gently kissed her neck and shoulder.

"Admit it; you want me."

"I can be surprisingly cooperative when necessary," she replied in a soft tone.

Vahn groaned, took her right wrist in his hand, and spun her around, placing her back to the wall while again pinning her body with his. He recaptured her left wrist and held both to the wall near her head, allowing his fingers to intertwine with hers. He looked into her eyes and kept his lips close to hers while grinning deviously. Vahn brushed his lips past hers, withholding the kiss he desperately desired. Jade silently lifted her foot from the water and tapped her heel against the wall behind her. A two-inch spike appeared from the tip of her shoe. One kick in the right spot and she would end Vahn's criminal career.

"Unfortunately," he announced then turned serious, "I need to get you out of here before Cody realizes what I've done."

Jade hesitated and stared at him with a surprised look. "What did you do?"

"Chose you over him, of course," he replied while grinning. "What else?"

Vahn quickly kissed her warmly but passionately on the mouth, pulling away before she could protest. Jade stared into his eyes a moment, then hesitated and touched her heel to the wall. The spike disappeared into her shoe. Vahn released her wrists then removed her gun from his pocket and extended it to her.

"I'm trusting you not to shoot me."

Jade took the .22 semiautomatic from him, debated whether or not she wanted to shoot him, and then returned the small gun to her thigh holster.

"There's a supply closet just past the stairs," he casually informed her. "It has a trapdoor in the ceiling. We can climb through that to the second-floor and escape down the fire escape. It's going to be pretty wild on the streets judging by the gunfire and sirens. We'll need to find shelter as quickly as possible."

"I know just where to go."

"Then we should get there."

"What about the bomb?" she demanded.

"It's not even connected," he informed her. "I'd never risk the lives of all those innocent people."

She was momentarily puzzled. Vahn took her free hand and hurried her toward the stairs.

Chapter Thirty-six

Bernard hurried through the rubble to join Cody near the bar, where he finished a glass of scotch. He looked at his man and frowned.

"Is it done?"

"He's gone."

Cody looked at Bernard and appeared confused then sedate. "Who's gone?"

"Our VIP guest," Bernard remarked then fidgeted. "Vahn's missing too."

Cody stared at him with surprise then attempted to control his emotions. "And Vahn's detective girlfriend?"

"Bruno said she was in the closet with our guest," Bernard informed him. "She's gone too."

"That son-of-a-bitch," Cody snarled and slammed his glass on the bar. "He must've made a deal with the detective. How is it he makes deals with his dick, and it somehow works out for him?"

"I couldn't say," Bernard replied then raised his brows. "What do you want to do? Should we search the place?"

"That would be pointless," Cody snarled and shook his head. "Somehow, he's already made it outside. I'd stake my life on it. How's the exit coming?"

"Just opened up," Bernard replied.

"And Jared?"

"First one out."

"Figures," Cody scoffed. "I need you to make sure everyone gets out of here. I'll take Bruno outside and search for Vahn and our VIP guest. If you see either, you know what to do."

Bernard nodded.

§

Jade and Vahn hurried to the supply room in the nearby corridor not far from the main floor within the nightclub. When they entered, Greg jumped with a startled cry. Vahn aimed his gun at Greg. Jade aimed her gun at Vahn. He tensed and cast a look at the gun she had aimed at his head. She snatched the gun from his hand.

"Sorry, Vahn," she replied with little emotion. "I don't exactly trust you."

Greg sighed with relief. "Thank God for that."

"You can either stay here or come along with us," Jade informed him with little emotion, "but if you're coming along, you'll do so without your weapon."

He casually turned to face her and eyed the gun she kept trained on him. "Obviously, I'm going with you."

Jade lowered her gun and motioned Greg to the crawl space opening. He climbed the shelf, opened the panel, and easily crawled through. Jade placed Vahn's gun down the front of her dress and returned her small pistol to her thigh holster. She then climbed up the shelf after Greg. Vahn casually looked up her dress as she crawled through the opening.

"Hmm," he announced while grinning his approval as he climbed the shelf behind her. "Black thong. Very nice."

As he followed after her through the opening, she thrust her high heel toward his face, sending a warning message. He dodged the high heel then grinned and continued through the opening behind her. Greg, Jade, and Vahn carefully walked along the remaining second floor and observed the large chunk of floor missing toward the middle. The area they walked across seemed stable enough, although made each a little tense. They entered a small, empty room and saw the open window on the opposite end. They approached the window and crawled through it onto the fire escape.

A few minutes after they had passed through the window, Miller stepped into the same room and looked around. He then continued toward the main area of the second-floor. The large opening in the floor was heart stopping. He noticed the open crawl space door and headed for it, climbing down into the storage closet. He then headed through the back corridor and entered the club, which was left in complete shambles. He scanned the area only a moment before he was nearly plowed down by Bruno as he hurried past him and toward the front of the club. There appeared to be no other signs of life. As Miller looked across the nightclub, he saw the last of the patrons crawling out the opening in the front with Bruno bringing up the rear. Miller scratched his head and continued to scan the club.

Chapter Thirty-seven

Vahn hurried Jade and Greg to the expensive, dirt coated Bentley with its hubcaps missing. They could see the other patrons exiting the building through the small, cleared opening that used to be the door. Jade saw Miller's car parked on the main road and did a quick scan for her partner. When she didn't' see him, she cursed softly. She wanted to look for him, but she knew they were in trouble if Cody discovered Greg was missing. Jade jumped in the front passenger side while Greg dove into the back. Vahn frantically searched the glove compartment for the spare keys. Cody now stood outside the club just near the alleyway and saw them attempting to escape in his Bentley. He slapped his men and indicated his car within the alley. His men ran down the alley after them.

Vahn thrust the car into gear and floored the gas pedal. The Bentley took off down the alley in the opposite direction. Vahn drove along the cluttered road, weaving in and out of crashed cars and fissures in the road. All three marveled at the disaster surrounding them. There was mass destruction, fires, and gangs shooting at one another while the police attempted to control the situation. Another car soon appeared behind them. Vahn looked in the rearview mirror and frowned, knowing who was in the car behind them. Jade and Greg stared out the back while Vahn drove at high speeds despite the road conditions.

"We need to lose them," Jade exclaimed.

"I'm working on it," he grumbled. "There's a bit more road hazards than there were earlier."

"And if we lose them, where do we go?" Greg demanded. "This city looks like a war zone."

"We need to get that information from your computer," Jade announced to Greg.

"Then we need to get to my computer," Greg informed her. "I can't access it remotely. That computer geek has a firewall even I can't hack."

"So if Cody gets to your computer first, there's no way to get that information?" Jade asked with concern.

"None at all," Greg replied while nervously fidgeting in the back seat. "And if he destroys my computer, it's gone forever. Of course, so is his money."

"So he won't destroy your computer?"

"No more than he'd kill me," Greg informed her. "He needs us both."

Jade turned to Vahn in the driver's seat and stared at him with a serious look. "You need to lose them," she announced then eyed him sharply with irritation. "I thought this was what you did for a living?"

"Kicking me in my boys is one thing, princess, but insulting my driving won't be tolerated."

"Maybe you should have let me drive," she scoffed and raised a demanding brow.

Vahn groaned with irritation. "That's it," he snarled. "See if you get any tonight." He then nodded, indicating his gun down the front of her dress. "You have my gun. Impress me by shooting out their tires."

Jade considered the request then rolled down her window and kneeled on the car seat while leaning out the window. Both Vahn and Greg eyed her backside in the short dress. Vahn removed his cell phone from his inner jacket pocket and took a picture. Jade fired at the car behind them. The Bentley drove around the wrecked cars at high speeds with the other car chasing after them. Jade fired twice and missed, unable to hit her target due to their weaving in and out of obstacles. She fired again, hitting the car's front tire, causing it to slide out of control and strike a parked car. Jade slid back into the seat with a satisfied grin.

"That was kind of fun," she announced cheerfully.

Vahn grinned but didn't comment.

Greg poked his head between the two seats. "He took a picture of your ass."

Vahn threw his hand back, backhanding Greg in the mouth. He clutched his mouth and fell to the back seat. Jade glared at Vahn with irritation while Vahn glared at Greg in the back seat.

"What's wrong with you?" Vahn snarled at Greg.

"I asked you to let me see it," he pouted while holding his mouth.

Jade glared at Vahn and extended her hand. "Give me the phone."

"It's in my pants."

Jade felt his pants pockets for his cell phone.

Vahn grinned slyly. "No, I mean it's really *in* my pants."

Jade eyed his pants, saw the outline of the cellphone not far from his crotch then frowned and looked away.

Vahn chuckled without looking at her. "Come on," he teased. "Where's your sense of adventure?"

Chapter Thirty-eight

The remaining sixteen Virtual Play employees stood within cubicle square and listened to the sound of banging coming from the fire doors. Larson motioned for everyone to hide. Everyone dove beneath whatever desks were still standing. The sound of a shotgun blast frightened everyone. Abby gasped from beneath the desk then covered her mouth to keep quiet. Three punks in their late teens to early twenties ran into the office toting shotguns and handguns. They ripped out computers and tossed them into a mail cart they rolled behind them. They laughed and hollered like psychotic demons then shot random monitors with the shotgun just to watch them shatter. When the monitor on the desk above her shattered, Janice screamed. One of the interlopers rounded the desk, grabbed her by the arm, and pulled her out from under the desk.

"Look," the first punk announced while cackling. "We got a live one for target practice."

Peterson suddenly leaped out from beneath his desk behind them and ran for the lobby doors.

The second punk turned with his shotgun and grinned. "Rabbit season--"

He fired the shotgun, hitting Peterson in the back. Peterson took the full impact of both barrels and fell while running. Janice screamed hysterically.

"Oh, shut her up," the third punk lashed out. "I hate it when they scream."

The first punk aimed his gun at Janice and tightened his finger on the trigger. Dani grabbed the chair in front of where she hid, dived on top of it, and barreled forward riding the chair. She crashed into the punk, knocking him to the floor. The gun went off and the bullet struck the ceiling, knocking down more debris. Janice again screamed, now hysterical. Larson tackled Janice to the floor before the first punk could recover while the second punk aimed his shotgun at Dani.

"Not very smart," the second punk informed her.

Dani stared at the shotgun with a look of horror, awaiting the loud explosion of both barrels firing. Instead, they heard the soft ding of the elevator. Oddly enough, the sound was almost deafening in the heat of the moment. All eyes suddenly turned to the supposedly locked out elevator just beyond the glass lobby doors. The elevator doors opened to reveal Rafael in his trench coat while looking down at his cell phone, as he usually did when he arrived. He looked up with surprise to see the three armed punks holding Dani. Dani saw Rafael and stared at him with horror at what was about to unfold.

Rafael stared at the tense scene as his mouth fell open and he seemed to freeze. "Oops, wrong floor."

The second punk turned the shotgun away from Dani and aimed it at Rafael. Rafael raised an Uzi hidden beneath his trench coat and rapidly fired at the punk holding the shotgun, striking him several times before his bullet-riddled body was thrown to the floor. The other two intruders reacted and simultaneously aimed their weapons at him. Rafael leaped out of the elevator and rolled across the floor as they shot into the elevator, peppering it with shotgun pellets. Rafael popped up from alongside the front desk and fired at both men with a sweeping motion, mowing both down with multiple shots. Rafael slowly straightened and dropped his backpack to the floor. The first punk writhed around the floor while clutching his bleeding abdomen and gasped. Rafael walked past him and casually shot him in the head as he passed.

He looked around cubicle square and shook his head. "This place is a mess."

The others slowly came out from hiding. Abby and Larson checked on Peterson but didn't get very close before assessing his condition. Both cringed and looked away. Dani hurried for Rafael while sighing with relief, threw her arms around his neck, and hugged him.

"Thank God you happened along," she practically sobbed while clinging to him.

Rafael clung to her as if he'd never let go. Dani hesitated then slowly pulled away and met his gaze with a strange realization. He avoided looking at her.

Her eyes widened as she stared at him. "Boyd?" she suddenly gasped.

Rafael still didn't look at her. Dani smiled and again threw her arms around him, clung to him, and sobbed softly. Rafael held her and closed his eyes.

"Oh, my God," Abby gasped with surprise. "Boyd is the computer repair guy?"

"The Uzi toting computer repair guy," Larson muttered.

Dani pulled away while staring into Rafael's eyes and gently touched his face.

He still had some difficulty looking at her. "Sorry if you're disappointed."

Dani smiled, laughed joyfully, and kissed him quickly on the lips. Rafael appeared surprised. She pulled back and met his gaze while shaking her head.

"No, I'm not disappointed at all," she announced happily. "I'm glad it was you."

Rafael appeared relieved and smiled. Dani kissed him again but longer and with more passion. He returned the kiss without hesitation.

"Sorry for not being a true romantic here, but there's a war going on outside, and it's making its way into the building," Larson informed them. "We're not exactly safe."

Rafael released Dani and grabbed his backpack. "So let's level the playing field." He dumped nearly a dozen handguns and boxes of bullets onto the nearby desk.

Janice stared at the assortment of weapons and ammunition. "Where did you get these?"

"My niece's apartment," Rafael casually replied. "There's enough of us to defend this floor until the National Guard takes the city back."

"That elevator was locked out in the lobby," Larson remarked. "How did you use it?"

He eyed Larson with little reaction. "I picked the lock with my pen," Rafael remarked while loading magazines. "It's not exactly rocket science." He slapped the magazine into the semiautomatic and handed it to Abby.

Abby uncertainly accepted the weapon, stared at it a moment, and then glanced at him. "Who's your niece? Where did she get all these weapons?"

"The girl has some strange hobbies," Rafael informed Abby then considered the comment. "Maybe she and I aren't so different after all."

Once everyone was able to calm their nerves with a bottle of gin they'd found in one of the desk drawers, they covered Peterson's body. The remaining employees hunkered down for the evening, hoping to avoid further incidents from the war raging on the city streets. Rafael and Dani sat on the floor behind her desk, their backs to the partition wall and a gun alongside each of them. Dani was content to cling to Rafael's arm and rest her head on his shoulder. She was exhausted from everything that had happened in the last twelve hours. Rafael sent a text message on his cell phone, checked for a response, and then returned it to his jacket pocket with a low, disgusted groan.

"Who are you texting?" Dani asked.

"My niece," he replied with a sigh. "I haven't heard from her since the earthquake."

"I assume she wasn't at her apartment when you went for her weapons," Dani remarked and gave him a curious look. "Where do you think she went?"

"Club Zen."

"Club Zen?" Dani remarked with surprise. "That's the second time that place was mentioned today. Earlier--" She hesitated and considered the comment.

"Yes, my niece is Detective Wesson," he replied with a gentle sigh then stared at the damaged drop ceiling. "With all the damage and violence in the streets, she could have been called to duty. She could be anywhere in this crazy city." He was silent a moment then drew a deep, tense breath. "A lot of cops died tonight. They're not releasing names just yet. With the phones down, they're probably unable to notify relatives." He frowned. "The one phone call I fear more than any other."

"I'm sure she's okay, Rafael," Dani informed him while gently placing her hand on his arm. "Detective Wesson seems very, uh, capable."

"She's reckless," he scoffed and frowned with disapproval. "She thinks she's shielded by a field of invincibility. I swear she thinks she's James Bond."

"Is she?"

He eyed her with a bewildered look, uncertain of the question. "Is she what?"

"Is she James Bond?"

Rafael considered the question then cocked his head with a strange realization. "You know, she just might be." He managed a tiny smile and snorted a laugh. "The crazy girl is probably enjoying herself. She has a strange idea of a good time."

Chapter Thirty-nine

Jade and Greg clung to the inside of the Bentley and screamed with horror as Vahn took the hairpin curve without touching the brakes. It was hard to see the road beyond the debris, fissures, and crashed vehicles.

"Car! Car! Car!" Jade shouted while clinging to the door and her seat.

"I see the car!"

The Bentley slid in a complete circle, leaving a thick black layer of tire rubber, then stopped, jolting the passengers. Vahn missed hitting the wrecked car by inches. Jade and Greg clung to the inside of the car and breathed heavily from their wild ride.

Vahn eyed them and grinned. "Good tires," he informed them. "That's the secret to safe driving."

Jade eyed him while panting. "And anyone but you behind the wheel!"

"I'm going to be sick," Greg gasped and held his stomach.

Vahn eyed him through the rearview mirror. "Just keep it back there." He glanced at Jade and raised his brows. "Now, if the two of you don't mind, I'll decide what route to take."

"How the hell was I supposed to know there was a canyon in the middle of Fifth Avenue?" Greg demanded hotly in his own defense.

"I think I should drive," Jade chimed in.

Vahn stepped on the gas, rocketing the car forward while squealing the tires. Greg and Jade flew back against their seats, barely able to scream.

"This is my last time driving an expensive car like this," he informed her. "I'm milking it for all it's worth."

§

Dani and Rafael remained comfortably seated behind the desk with their backs to the partition. Rafael held her hand and gently played with it. Dani studied him while he caressed her hand with an odd seriousness.

"Why didn't you want me to know it was you?" she finally asked.

"Look at me then look at you," he replied while looking up and met her gaze. "You're young and beautiful. I'm kidding myself when I say I'm 5'8". I'm close to fifteen years older than you and, well, I look like a Muppet."

She suddenly blushed with embarrassment, having forgotten that little blunder. "I didn't mean that in a bad way. Muppets are cute." Dani turned on her hip to face him while clinging to his hand. "I always thought you were very attractive. Sure, I'd envisioned Boyd as a twenty-two-year-old, six-foot-something Greek god, but it's all those conversations we had that made me want Boyd." She offered a timid smile. "Not because I thought he was tall." She shrugged with some embarrassment. "I've never been out with a man who talked the way you do, with your intelligence. I only ever seem to attract the party animals." She laughed softly. "Trust me, once the party is over, there's nothing left but a mess to clean."

"I just didn't want to disappoint you, but mostly I didn't want our chats to end," he informed her in a timid tone. "I don't get out much. If it wasn't for Jade's constant prodding, I'd still be sitting at my kitchen table feeling sorry for myself. I need to be saved from me."

"I want to continue our chats, but I think I'd like to do them face-to-face, if that's okay with you," Dani informed him and gently squeezed his hand.

He stared into her eyes while caressing her hand. "I'd like that."

She fidgeted slightly while staring at him. "I hope you don't think me too forward--"

Dani leaned closer to Rafael and kissed him warmly but passionately on the lips. Rafael was slightly surprised but showed little hesitation as he pulled her into his arms and returned the kiss.

Chapter Forty

The Bentley pulled up to Jade's apartment overtop a used bookstore. The surrounding area was dark, but there didn't appear to be nearly as much damage in her neighborhood. Vahn and Greg followed Jade into her studio apartment where only a few items were scattered along the floor. Greg collapsed on her sofa and immediately shut his eyes.

"Don't get comfortable," she warned. "I'm just going to change and grab some weapons for our trip."

"It seems pretty safe here," Greg remarked and eyed her. "Maybe we should just wait for the National Guard to sweep and clean first. You know, get a couple of winks in."

Vahn grinned at her and teased, "Or maybe a shower for two."

Jade glared at Vahn, hoping her look would silence him. He eyed her, raised his brows suggestively, and grinned. She looked back at Greg.

"Cody knows I have you, so he'll eventually show up here looking for us," she informed him while folding her arms across her chest. "Even worse; if he gets to your computer first, we have nothing on him, and you remain a target."

"That would be a valid point, but I doubt he knows I need my computer," Greg replied.

"That's the plan," she informed them, leaving no room for argument. "I'm going to change. Stay here."

Jade disappeared into the nearby bedroom and shut the door behind her. Vahn glanced around the apartment and appeared deep in thought as if considering his options.

"She didn't lock the door," he remarked to Greg and raised a curious brow. "Think that means something?"

Greg rolled his eyes then smirked sarcastically. "Yeah, she's totally inviting you into her room," he replied. "You should take her up on the invitation or risk insulting her."

"That's what I thought too."

As Vahn approached the bedroom door, Greg hid his smile and tried to keep from laughing. While Jade was changing out of her black dress, the bedroom door unexpectedly opened and Vahn entered. Jade gasped with surprise and straightened, allowing him a generous view of her in just her black bra, thong panties, and thigh gun holster strapped to her leg and hip like some bizarre garter belt.

Vahn stood in the doorway and stared with more than a passing interest. "Oh, wow--"

Jade's embarrassment quickly turned to hostility. She spun into a roundhouse kick and struck him in the chest, throwing him against the door causing it to slam shut.

Vahn gingerly rubbed his chest. "Thanks for taking off the heels that time."

Jade threw a punch at his face. He dodged her punch but was struck with her left foot, kicking him in the shoulder. Vahn darted across the room and held up his hands defensively.

"Okay, I get it," he announced, attempting to calm her. "Not locking the door wasn't an invite."

"There is no lock on the door," she lashed out. "I'm sick and tired of you treating me like your wet dream! So from now on, I'll speak in a language you actually understand!"

Jade threw her body into a roundhouse kick. Vahn dove from her path and onto her bed, bouncing slightly.

"Hmm. Nice, firm mattress--"

Jade again kicked at him. He rolled across the bed and to his feet on the opposite side. Jade jumped onto the bed in a standing position and kicked for his head. He bolted from her path and ran around the foot end of the bed. Jade leaped off the bed, caught onto him, and flipped him with her body on the way down to the floor. Vahn landed roughly on his back with Jade landing on top straddling him.

"Okay," he announced with noted concern in his tone. "Maybe I've been a bit sexually aggressive--"

Jade punched him in the face. Vahn groaned painfully. She threw another punch. Vahn gasped, blocked her fist, and flipped her onto her back, placing himself on top. Jade attempted to punch him again. He caught her wrists, stopping her assault, and panted from the excessive workout.

"Okay, I'll admit I've been *very* sexually aggressive," he announced. "Let me apologize."

Jade glared at him with hostility but stopped struggling to hear him out.

Vahn eyed her and suddenly groaned. "This is exactly how I envisioned our honeymoon."

Jade thrust her knee into his hip, forcing him to yelp and loosen his grip. She flipped him roughly onto his back while again straddling him and slammed his wrists to the floor on either side of his head. The door opened to reveal Greg. He eyed them, appeared embarrassed, and smiled.

"Sorry," Greg announced while hiding his grin. "Just take your time."

Once Greg shut the door, Jade coiled back with her knee to kick Vahn in the groin.

Vahn appeared alarmed and gasped. "No, no, not that!"

As he pinched his eyes shut and braced for impact, Jade stopped and stared at him while breathing heavily. Vahn slowly opened his eyes and appeared relieved.

"I'm sorry. I'm sorry for all the remarks," he announced with sincerity. "I'm just very attracted to you, and I know I don't have a shot. I'm sure there's some sort of psychobabble bullshit term for what's wrong with me."

She slowly released his wrists and straightened on her knees while still straddling his hips. Vahn slowly sat up as Jade was about to move off him. He looked at her position over him and her lacy bra. He suddenly grabbed her under her buttocks with his arm, pulled her forward against him, and kissed her passionately and aggressively. Jade gasped with surprise and pushed against him. He broke off the kiss and met her gaze, searching her eyes.

"You can beat me up and flatten my boys," he announced, "but it was totally worth it."

Jade stared at him with an oddly annoyed look. He still held her hips against him and stared into her eyes with a serious look. Jade remained still and stared back at him. She relaxed her hands once braced against his chest and allowed her hand to caress his face. Vahn groaned softly then ran his hand along her bare back and caressed her buttocks with the other. He slowly moved his mouth closer to hers and kissed her warmly and with less aggression. She returned the kiss then immediately broke it off and attempted to pull away from him.

"We need to go," she announced.

"We have twenty minutes," he protested.

She stared at him with an unpredictable look. "You've got fifteen."

Vahn realized what she'd said then groaned and kissed her passionately with aggression. Jade immediately returned the kiss and savagely helped him out of his jacket and shoulder holster.

Chapter Forty-one

Greg opened a bottle of water while relaxing on the sofa within Jade's living room area. He then heard loud thumping and moaning coming from the bedroom. Greg eyed the bedroom door and shook his head.

"There's some strange bedfellows," he muttered.

Within the bedroom, Jade and Vahn aggressively groped each other beneath the sheets with Vahn on top of her. He moved against her with uninhibited passion. Jade suddenly flipped him onto his back, reversing their positions, and pinned his wrists to the mattress, holding him down.

Vahn groaned and smiled as Jade aggressively moved against him. "Oh, you're a dirty cop."

Back in the living room, Greg relaxed on the sofa and played a game of solitaire on his cell phone. Loud thumping and both male and female screams came from the bedroom. Greg attempted to drown out the sound by increasing the volume on music playing from his cell phone.

"Jesus Christ!" Vahn screamed loud enough to startle Greg despite the increased volume on his cell phone.

Greg rolled his eyes and sank into the sofa while attempting to concentrate on his game.

Back in the bedroom, Vahn suddenly tackled Jade to the bed, pinning her beneath him while panting and smiling.

"That was very un-ladylike," he teased.

Jade smiled while panting and ran her hands firmly along his shoulders. "You needed to be spanked," she announced then whispered something in his ear.

He suddenly groaned with pleasure and rolled his eyes shut. "Oh, yeah--"

Back in the living room, Greg sat on the sofa holding pillows over his ears while attempting to block out the noise. Despite the pillows against his ears, Jade was heard crying out with ecstasy while Vahn grunted and groaned. The bed struck the wall harshly and repeatedly in rhythm with their groaning. It sounded as if the headboard would knock down the wall. Greg held his breath and shut his eyes.

"My God," he groaned softly. "Finish her off already."

Within the bedroom, Jade and Vahn finally collapsed together on the bed. They clung to each other while panting heavily with exhaustion.

Vahn grinned while attempting to catch his breath. "That was the best twenty minutes of my life," he informed her. "I think I'm having a heart attack."

"Maybe next time you shouldn't drive the headboard through the wall."

He suddenly smiled and cast a look at her in his arms. "You'll give me a next time?"

Jade fell silent, avoided looking at him, and nestled her head against his chest. "Well, I wouldn't mind having a chance for an orgasm."

"What are you talking about?" he suddenly proclaimed. "I counted at least three."

"Hmm--no."

He stared at the top of her head a moment with surprise or possible horror. "Come on," he nearly exploded. "That was definitely the sounds of a woman having an orgasm."

"I'm afraid not," she replied while hiding her smile. "That was just having fun."

"Having fun? I worked my ass off for those screams," he insisted in protest. "You could at least have let me believe I did that."

"You did," she replied casually. "It just wasn't what you thought."

"Does the whole building complain about the noise when you get off?" he scoffed.

Jade half lay on him and met his gaze while her grin mocked him. "Getting me off requires a lot of prep work and more than twenty minutes."

He appeared to sulk then looked determined. "I want a rematch," Vahn insisted proudly. "You're not getting away with this. Total injustice."

Jade returned her head to his chest and clung to him. Her smile slowly faded when she realized what she'd actually done.

"This should never have happened," she remarked in a timid tone.

"Why?" he asked. "Because you think I'm a hitman for the mob?"

"Exactly."

"I keep telling you, I'm not a hitman," he informed her then considered the comment, "but I'm not a choir boy either."

"So what are you?"

"Misguided and looking for a second chance at life and love," he replied.

Jade moved onto her elbow and met his gaze. "That might be out of my hands."

"I know," he warmly replied then pulled her against him and kissed her passionately.

Vahn walked out of the bedroom while buttoning his shirt. He saw Greg staring at him with a serious look on his face and his mouth hanging partway open.

Vahn glared back at him with irritation. "What?"

"I can't believe you got her off three times," Greg gasped with astonishment. "You're, like, my hero. She looked like a tough customer too."

Vahn seemed to consider the comment then smiled, pleased with himself. "What can I say? She's hot for me."

"Son-of-a-bitch!" Jade screamed from the bedroom, alarming both men.

Vahn and Greg ran into the bedroom. They discovered Jade, now dressed combat ready and wearing her leather jacket, standing in front of her closet door. She stared into the half-empty gun cabinet located within her closet.

"What's wrong?" Vahn asked.

"That bastard took half my guns," she cried out then looked around the gun cabinet. "He took my Uzi!"

"What bastard?" Greg asked.

"My uncle!" Jade removed two guns and some ammunition. "Left me all the crappy weapons. Who does he think he is? Dirty Quinn?"

Greg patted Vahn on the back. "She's all yours, man."

Vahn grinned lustfully while folding his arms across his chest as he leaned in the doorway. "She's a keeper all right," he announced. "A woman with an Uzi. That's so hot."

Greg rolled his eyes and walked away. "Get help. Please."

Chapter Forty-two

Dani and Rafael sat behind the desk and listened to the sound of repetitive gunfire coming from outside the building. It sounded close, possibly just outside the lobby. There was no telling what was going on within the city streets, and it was unwise to stand near the mostly shattered windows. Although they were up high enough to avoid any issues with those on the ground, aftershocks could take out the side of the building.

"Do you think that's the National Guard?" Dani asked while clinging to Rafael's arm.

"No, I don't."

Rafael grabbed the discarded Uzi and sprang to his feet. Dani grabbed her semiautomatic and joined him. Larson, Brad, and another man hurried into the open office door and looked outside where the parking garage used to be.

"There's a lot of gunfire coming from the lobby. I doubt it's the police. Sounds like a war going on down there." Larson eyed Rafael. "What do you think?"

"Rival gangs settling old scores," Rafael remarked.

"What's our next move?" Larson asked while seeking Rafael's input on their situation.

Dani thought it seemed odd that Larson was suddenly turning over control to the man who repairs computers. Was Larson losing faith in his own abilities to lead?

"If we're lucky they'll give up at the barricaded doors, but we need to be prepared," Rafael informed him. "Let's move some of the desks in front of the lobby door and the glass wall to seal it. If they break through the fire door, breaking the glass and climbing over the desks will leave any intruders exposed. We'll be able to pick them off before they make it past the barricade."

Larson nodded in agreement and rallied the others. They moved several desks in front of the glass wall and lobby door. Another group moved desks from the cubicles to form a second barrier before cubicle square. Janice and Abby moved another desk in front of one of the offices in the back as a last resort. The office was big enough that those remaining could barricade themselves inside if it came to that. The sound of gunfire echoed from the first floor. Everyone remained positioned safely behind the desks and clung to their weapons.

"My God, listen to it down there," Dani gasped while trembling. "It sounds like a war."

"If we're lucky, they'll kill one another," Rafael muttered while staring at the barricaded glass.

The gunfire ceased within the lobby, although shots could still be heard in the distance coming from the city streets. Everyone listened in silence. They could hear faint footfalls of someone within the stairwell. Rafael, who was positioned behind the receptionist's desk on the front line with Larson, looked at the others behind the second barricade.

"Someone's coming," Rafael announced to the others. "Second-string, if they get through the barricaded stairwell door, don't shoot until we're out of the way."

They nodded and remained ready but nervous. Rafael, Larson, and Brad focused on the hallway just beyond the glass lobby wall. They heard pounding on the stairwell door. The pounding stopped, leaving an eerie silence. For a moment, it was possible that the intruders gave up and went to another floor. They heard the blast of a shotgun as the door flew open. Everyone jumped and ducked behind their barricades. The three men behind the receptionist desk kept their weapons aimed while remaining shielded behind the tall desk. They didn't see anyone, and nothing moved beyond the glass. Jade dived through the broken glass over the desk, rolled across the floor, and popped up in a crouched position with her semiautomatic aimed.

Rafael stared at the armed woman with surprise. "Don't shoot," he cried out.

Jade remained motionless with her gun aimed and assessed the situation. Rafael slowly stood with his hands up while holding the Uzi.

"Jade--?"

She appeared relieved and lowered her gun. Rafael ran around the desk, approached Jade, and pulled her into his arms. She returned the loving embrace.

"I'm so glad you're okay," she whispered near his ear while clinging to him.

Their joyful reunion ended abruptly when Jade pulled away, glared at him, and snatched the Uzi.

"I can't believe you took my Uzi," she lashed out and waved the weapon. "You never touch a woman's Uzi!"

"Sorry."

Vahn hurried Greg into the lobby then over the second barricade of desks to cubical square. The other employees saw Greg and commented quietly among themselves. Jade climbed over the desk and allowed Vahn to assist her down to the other side. His hand caressed her buttocks as he released her. She frowned and swatted angrily at his hand. Vahn grinned playfully. Rafael saw their interaction and glared his disapproval.

Greg hurried to his office and barely looked back as he spoke. "I'll need at least thirty minutes," he announced.

Janice and Abby shouted a warning as he opened his office door. Greg stared at the dark, empty space that was once his office and the parking garage.

"Holy shit! What happened to my office?"

Jade and Vahn joined Greg in the doorway and stared at the mound of rubble.

"That's going to slow things down," Vahn commented while folding his arms across his chest.

"It's gone! My computer is gone," he cried out. "All the evidence I had on Cody--"

"Look on the bright side," Vahn announced and playfully slapped him on the back. "With his billions lost, he has no reason to torture you."

"Yeah, he'll just shoot me instead," Greg snapped back and pulled away from Vahn.

"I didn't say it was perfect," Vahn casually replied.

Greg glared at Vahn, obviously not humored, then shook his head and groaned. "I need a minute," he muttered. "If you need me, I'll be in the bathroom."

Jade and Vahn looked into the vast nothingness that was once Greg's office. They stared out at the dark city as sirens continued to wail.

"This is just great," Jade remarked.

"Greg!" Larson cried out.

Jade and Vahn turned in time to see Greg leaping over the desk barricade and taking off for the fire stairs.

"Damn it," Jade cried out and was about to run after him and bring him back.

"I'll get him," Larson announced and took off after the fleeing programmer.

Rafael stood behind Jade and noted her frazzled look. "What's going on?"

She turned to face her uncle and groaned with defeat. If she ever got her hands on Greg, she'd almost certainly punch him or worse.

"Greg had evidence on his computer to put away Cody Riley, but it appears his computer is gone forever," she informed her uncle while frowning. "The bastard took off in the interest of saving his own ass."

"You don't need the computer," Rafael informed her with little concern. "All that information is on the main server. You just need to access it from another unit."

"I'm afraid not," she informed him. "Greg didn't put it on the secured server because he didn't want anyone else having access to the information. That's why he needed his computer."

"I can understand why you would assume that," Rafael replied, "but when I was in his computer to do updates, I saved those files to the server."

She stared at him with surprise.

He casually shrugged. "I thought it might be something important, so I took additional steps to ensure it could be recovered if the police needed it."

"You can access it from another unit?" Jade gasped.

"No, you can't access it," Brad suddenly chimed in. "If you saved it to the server from Greg's computer, it went into his account. He did something to his account to prevent anyone including administrators from accessing his work. Untrusting bastard."

"How do you know that?" Dani asked with surprise.

Brad fidgeted slightly. "I may have tried to hack into his account once. I'm telling you, it can't be hacked."

"Maybe you can't hack into his account on the server," Rafael announced casually, "but I can."

Jade looked around at the remaining workers, her anxiety rising. "Find him a working computer!"

Everyone searched the office for a working computer. Larson returned a few minutes later, having been unsuccessful in his hunt for

Greg. He immediately helped search for working computer parts. They found parts from different computers and piled them on one of the desks. Rafael attached the keyboard, mouse, and monitor to the tower then pulled a chair before the desk and began typing. Everyone watched Rafael's fingers fly along the keyboard. The monitor revealed different screens that appeared to pop up and vanish rapidly.

"Holy shit! Look at him go," Janice gasped.

"I practically paid for college typing other student's papers," Rafael remarked.

"How can you even see what the screen says?" Vahn asked while staring over his shoulder.

"I don't have to; I know what it says," Rafael informed him without taking his eyes off the screen. He grinned deviously. "I love hacking secured servers." He continued to work while barely casting a glance at Jade. "What do I do with the information once I retrieve it?"

"Can you save it to a flash drive?" Jade asked.

"If you find me a flash drive."

Everyone searched the trashed cubicle square for a flash drive. They routed through drawers and sifted through debris on the floor. Dani finally found one and hurried to the desk.

"I found one," Dani cried out as she approached, "but I don't know how much space is available on it."

Rafael took the stick without missing a stroke and inserted it into the computer. The flash drive contents appeared then disappeared as if by magic.

Larson hurried back to the desk with a concerned look on his face. "There's someone coming up the stairs," he announced to the others. "With the stairway door wide open, they're just going to walk right in."

Vahn and Jade grabbed their weapons and hurried for Dani's desk. Someone fired at them. Everyone took cover except Rafael, who was partially shielded behind the divider wall in cubicle square. Dani crouched alongside Rafael's chair and watched him work without appearing distracted by the gunfire. She held her gun and kept watch on the lobby. Jade and Vahn fired back into the hallway. A smoke bomb suddenly flew into the lobby. Everyone screamed and scattered. Smoke quickly filled the area behind the desk. Rafael continued to type. Dani kept her gun aimed despite the smoke filtering from the lobby into cubicle square. Cody, Bruno, and four other men shoved the desk aside and filed into the room like a mini SWAT team. Both sides fired their weapons.

"You have to take cover, Rafael," Dani cried out, concerned for his safety.

"I'm in," he cried out. "Watch my back."

"He's accessing the files," Cody shouted from across the room, although he couldn't get past the second barricade of armed workers to stop him.

Rafael hit the button and removed the flash drive. He stood and looked at Jade.

"Jade!"

She turned to see Rafael with the flash drive. He threw her the stick and tackled Dani to the floor as Cody's men shot at him. Jade caught the stick, diverting their attention to her instead. Vahn stared at the stick in her hand and appeared alarmed. He pushed Jade across the lobby and over the desk toward the elevator.

"Go!" he shouted.

Jade ran for the elevator with Vahn behind her, firing shots at Cody and his men, forcing them to take cover behind the desk in front of the lobby doorway. Jade and Vahn dove into the safety of the elevator. Jade hit a button to release the elevator, allowing the doors to close. The men ran from the office except one who continued to shoot at the remaining workers. The office workers fired back. Larson's gun clicked empty, forcing him to dive behind a desk. Cody's man made it past the second barricade and aimed his gun at Rafael, who shielded Dani on the floor. Both stared at the man with horror. A gun fired. Rafael covered Dani. When he wasn't shot, Rafael slowly lifted his head and looked toward the shooter. Cody's man suddenly appeared motionless as blood seeped from his mouth. He then collapsed to the floor. Miller stood with his gun in hand on the other side of the second barricade then looked around while lowering his gun.

"Where's Jade?" Miller demanded.

Rafael jumped up from the floor and dove into his chair, riding it in front of the computer. "Running an errand." He resumed typing on the computer.

Dani appeared alarmed while staring at him with her mouth hanging open. "I thought you passed it off to Jade?" she gasped with surprise.

"I'm good, but I'm not that good," he informed her. "She's buying me time."

"Does she know that?" Dani cried out.

"That's irrelevant."

Dani considered their situation then straightened and looked at the others. "Find another flash drive!"

Chapter Forty-three

The elevator doors barely opened on the fifth floor when Vahn and Jade ran into the corridor. They heard thundering feet on the stairs not far from them and closing fast. Jade and Vahn ran along the hallway to the nearest door and bolted inside. They paused just inside the doorway and listened to the sound of running feet in the corridor. Jade leaned against the wall while clinging to her Uzi and the flash drive. She stuck the flash drive down her shirt into her cleavage for safekeeping. Vahn strained to see down her shirt then looked around the dimly lit television studio and appeared surprised to see the talk show set. Apart from television equipment laying smashed on the floor, the studio seemed to have suffered less damage than the ninth floor.

"Isn't this that show where those women sit around drinking coffee and gossiping about stuff no one cares about?" Vahn asked while raising a curious brow.

"I think so."

He frowned, obviously displeased with the response. "I really hate that show."

Vahn nudged Jade down the aisle of nearly one hundred stadium seats toward the stage with a desk and several toppled chairs. The show's coffee mugs with the show logo on them lay strewn along the desk. Jade and Vahn hurried across the stage and toward backstage, where more equipment lay scattered along the floor. The studio door behind them opened to reveal Bruno and another man, Fellows. Cody brought up the rear. Before the men could see them, Jade and Vahn hurried across backstage for another entrance. When they nearly reached the door, it opened. Vahn grabbed Jade and pulled her behind some fallen stage equipment. They both crouched down and silently watched the two men enter through the back door with their guns clutched in their hands. There were two in the front and two to their rear. Both were closing fast.

"Want to see stupidity at its finest?" Vahn asked while grinning deviously.

"You don't need to prove anything to me," she scoffed, mocking him.

"Funny."

Vahn picked up a ceramic mug from the floor, turned toward the studio door, and threw it across the room. It struck the door with a loud thud and shattered. Both men turned toward the studio door with their guns aimed. The door opened to reveal Fellows as the two men opened fire. Fellows took several hits before falling to the floor. The two men appeared horrified and ran for their fallen man. Vahn grinned and nudged Jade. She shook her head at the pride he displayed regarding the accidental shooting. She followed him toward the back door. While Bruno argued with the two men, Jade and Vahn slipped out. They entered the ladies restroom, seeking shelter.

Vahn looked around and appeared bewildered. "I thought this was the bathroom?"

"It is."

"No wonder women take so long in the bathroom," he remarked while scanning the room. "Look at this place. Perfume, make-up, mints--" He looked up with surprise. "My God, you have a television. Hell, I'd never leave the bathroom if I had one that looked like this."

"No one has a bathroom like this," she muttered. "Check out the one at the precinct. It's pretty disgusting."

"I've seen the men's room on numerous occasions, thank you," he replied. "So what's the plan? Are we going to hang out in here all night?"

"No, we need to get as far away from here as possible," she replied.

"If we try to make a run for it, we run the risk of Cody getting his hands on that flash drive," Vahn informed her then drew a deep breath and looked around. "We should just find a quiet place to hide until the National Guard arrives."

Jade subconsciously ran her fingers through her mussed hair. "There's nothing on the flash drive."

He stared at her with surprise. "What?"

"Congratulations, you're a decoy."

"A decoy?"

"Rafael's good, but he's not that good," she informed him. "There's no way he got the information onto this flash drive. He needed more time."

"You got all that from him throwing you a flash drive?" he demanded.

"No, but I know Rafael," she replied and frowned with defeat. "When he accomplishes something he knows no one else can, he gets this annoying smirk on his face. The look he gave me was frustrated."

"Great," Vahn huffed with a look of disgust on his face. "We're being hunted by the mob, and we don't even have anything worth bargaining."

"They don't know that," she informed him.

"I wish I didn't either," he muttered.

Chapter Forty-four

Cody paced the television studio stage while his remaining men searched the area. Bruno entered the studio and approached his boss. Cody turned and watched him walk down the steps toward him.

"Well?"

"We have the stairs blocked, and the elevator is in our line of sight," Bruno announced. "They can't leave this floor without us knowing."

"I want him found," Cody snarled then paced impatiently. "Who's left? We need additional men. Were you able to contact the others?"

"No," Bruno replied. "Phone lines are still jammed. I sent a text, but no one's responding."

"We can't let them out of this building with that flash drive," Cody informed his man with a moderately concerned look on his face. "If Jared finds out I lost his billions, I'm as good as dead." He eyed Bruno. "I think it's safe to assume everyone beneath me will go down with me."

Bruno frowned at the comment and shifted uncomfortably. "We'll find them."

"Yeah, or we're all dead," he remarked. "Kindly mention that to the guys, so they don't screw up, okay?"

§

*J*ade paced the bathroom while Vahn sat on the vanity and played with the basket of perfume and lipsticks. He checked each shade of lipstick and held a few to her for her approval. She glared at him and shook her head.

"Give it up," she snarled and returned to pacing. "I'm not wearing lipstick for you."

Vahn groaned and jumped to his feet. "Okay, so we need to leave the building. The stairwell is our best option," he informed her. "There's one about thirty feet from here to the right. If they're not in the hallway, they're going to be watching the stairwells. We need a plan."

"Really? If you've got one, I'd like to hear it."

"Of course I have a plan," he blurted out. "You need to buy Rafael time, and they want the flash drive. You give me the flash drive, and we'll cut them a deal for it."

"What? I'm not going to sell them the flash drive," she softly cried out.

"You're missing the point, Jade," he announced. "We sell them the flash drive; they leave the building. Rafael gets the information, and Cody goes to jail."

"And you're suddenly worth a couple of million?" she demanded with an arrogant look in her eyes.

"I didn't say it didn't have its perks," he announced while grinning then whined playfully. "Come on. He gives me the million, you come out smelling like a rose, and we dance off to Bora Bora."

"No, absolutely not."

He frowned his disapproval and shook his head. "You lack imagination, Jade."

"I don't take money from the mob, Vahn."

"You wouldn't," he corrected then grinned. "I would. How can you not like that plan?"

She glared at him.

He frowned and shook his head. "You're not really a 'see the bigger picture' sort of woman, are you?"

"When you come up with a good plan," she snarled. "Please let me know.

"You're no fun, Detective Wesson," Vahn informed her while shaking his head. "Our relationship can't revolve solely around sex, you know?"

Chapter Forty-five

Bruno stood by the doorway in the television studio with his gun in his hand while watching the stairway. Cody paced the area in the back behind the seats with an annoyed look on his face. Vahn suddenly appeared in the backstage doorway with his semiautomatic trained on them.

"Hey, Cody," Vahn chirped cheerfully.

Cody and Bruno spun with their guns aimed and were now locked in a standoff.

"Take it easy. Let's not do anything stupid," Vahn announced then grinned. "I want to make you a deal. I have something you want, and you have something I want."

"Typical," Cody scoffed. "What is it you want, Vahn?"

"I'm not greedy, Cody. I only want one million," he announced and mocked him with his smile. "I know you can spare it, especially since that flash drive tells you where the rest of the billions you stole from Jared have been moved."

"Give me one good reason why I should pay you a million dollars instead of just shooting you and taking the flash drive?" Cody demanded.

"Because it's not on me. Give me some credit for intelligence," he replied. "I've had plenty of time to hide it. It's someplace where you'll never find it."

"And what about your detective girlfriend?"

"Been there; done that," Vahn teased. "I can find a dozen more like her, especially with a million dollars in my pocket."

"Where is she?" Cody demanded.

He chuckled in his throat. "She's a little tied up at the moment."

Cody glared at Vahn as he approached the stage area from the back. "After the shit you pulled, do you actually expect me to believe you?"

"What? Helping her escape?" Vahn asked then grinned. "She had something I wanted." He considered the comment then chuckled. "Well, she had a couple of things I wanted. Access to a million dollars was motivation too."

"Okay, I'll give you your million dollars for the flash drive," Cody announced firmly then raised his brow, "and Detective Wesson."

"Why not?" Vahn announced and shrugged. "I'm finished with her anyway."

Vahn disappeared backstage then reappeared with Jade. Her wrists were tied in front of her, and she had duct tape across her mouth. Vahn ripped the duct tape from her mouth then tossed her across the floor, forcing her to land just behind the desk.

Jade managed to jump to her feet with her hostility showing. "You bastard!"

Jade attempted to karate kick him, despite her tied hands. Without flinching, Vahn raised the .22 semiautomatic in his left hand and casually shot her in the chest. She cried out and flew to the floor behind the desk. He tossed the .22 aside while keeping his 9mm in his right hand. Vahn looked back at Cody and appeared satisfied.

"Here's the deal," Vahn announced. "You and your brat pack walk out of here, you get my money, and I'll meet you in one hour at the docks."

"Fine. One hour," Cody snarled then pointed a warning finger at him. "But you had better be there with that flash drive."

Vahn waved them off then disappeared backstage. Cody didn't even give it a second thought before motioning Bruno to follow him. Bruno hurried past the seats toward the stage as Cody disappeared out the main entrance. As Bruno approached the dead woman and the backstage door, Jade suddenly kicked his legs out from under him, sprang to her feet while tossing the ropes aside, and kicked him as he stood. Vahn appeared from the stage door and watched as Jade kicked the large man several times.

Vahn smirked, pleased. "You are so hot."

She watched the big man fall to the floor then glared at Vahn. "I hope you realize how much being shot stings," she snapped hotly then rubbed her chest revealing the bulletproof vest.

"It was just a pussy .22 caliber," Vahn scoffed and rolled his eyes. "Grow a set."

Jade glared at him. He caught her look then smiled and chuckled.

"We'd better go," she announced. "We don't want to keep Cody's ambush waiting."

She again rubbed her chest then looked at her aunt's leather jacket. There was a bullet hole in the chest. She stopped and examined the hole straight through the jacket. Horror crossed her face as she glared at Vahn.

"You put a hole in my jacket," she cried out.

"Come on," Vahn groaned. "That jacket is old and ratty. So what if it has a bullet hole?"

"This was my aunt's jacket," Jade protested. "She gave it to me the day she died. I don't care if it's old and ratty."

Jade took off the jacket and examined the bullet hole that went straight through. She checked the liner, which ripped with little effort. Jade groaned and examined the rip.

"Great," she scoffed, feeling defeated. "Now I'll need to have it repaired."

Jade was about to slip into the jacket when a flash drive fell to the floor. Vahn and Jade stared at the flash drive.

"Want to be careful and not lose that," Vahn remarked. "We may need that as a bargaining chip."

She uncertainly picked up the flash drive, stared at it, and then looked at Vahn. Jade removed the flash drive Rafael gave her from her cleavage.

Vahn appeared puzzled and pointed. "I thought he only gave you one."

"He did," Jade remarked and studied the second flash drive. She then looked at the torn jacket and sank into thought. "It must have been in the lining of my jacket."

"Did it fall through a hole in your pocket?" Vahn asked. "Happens with my keys a lot."

Jade slowly shook her head. "No, I don't fiddle with computers," she replied. "I don't have any use for a flash drive." She then eyed Vahn. "It must have been my aunt's."

Vahn stared at her as she drifted into thought. Jade was taken back to the day her aunt gave her the jacket.

"Okay, so it was your aunt's," Vahn replied. "Does it matter? We should meet Cody's ambush before he decides to come back for us."

"Yeah, we will," she announced then looked around. "There has to be a computer around here somewhere."

"Why do we need a computer?" Vahn asked.

"I want to see what's on this flash drive," she replied. "I have this really weird feeling."

"If it's that important to you," he announced then pointed toward the door. "I saw an office down the hall."

As they hurried through the stage door, Jade stopped in the doorway and eyed Cody's man lying on the floor just inside the hall. Vahn casually stepped over him.

She glared at him with annoyance. "Did you ever meet anyone you didn't kill?"

"He's not dead."

"He looks dead."

Jade reached down to take the man's pulse. Before she could even touch his wrist, Vahn captured her arm and pulled her away from him.

"Okay, maybe he's dead," Vahn casually replied. "That was self-defense though. You've killed more people tonight than I have, so quit nitpicking."

Chapter Forty-six

Vahn opened the office door, allowing Jade to enter first. Jade looked around the dimly lit office and found a working light. The room brightened considerably. There wasn't a desktop computer, but she saw a laptop on the desk. Despite the messy state of the office, the laptop hadn't been crushed. Jade sat before the desk and checked the laptop. It still worked. She inserted the flash drive and opened it. Vahn stood over her shoulder and watched with mild disinterest.

"So what am I looking at?" he asked.

She saw there was only one file on the flash drive. Jade opened the file to reveal several smaller files. Jade stared at the files with some surprise.

"The files on this flash drive were created the day before my aunt died," Jade informed him then shook her head with disbelief. "The creator was Russ Thomas."

"Should I know who that is?" Vahn asked.

"Russ Thomas worked at my parents' accounting firm," she informed him. "He was accused of murdering his wife and her lover in a hotel room. He ran from the police and supposedly jumped to his death from the twelfth floor of the Strafford Hotel." She remained curious while opening the files. "Why did my aunt have a flash drive belonging to Russ in her jacket pocket?" As the file opened, Jade relived that day in her aunt's office. She suddenly sat forward and stared at the file. "I could be mistaken, but this looks a lot like blackmail."

Vahn looked at the computer screen. There were several pictures downloaded onto the flash drive file. As they flipped through them, they saw a series of events involving a much younger Cody and Jared Carmichael. Cody had a gun in his hand, and both men stood over two dead men with bullet holes in the backs of their skulls and a pool of blood surrounding their heads. Cody and Jared were smiling and laughing despite the grisly scene.

"That's Cody," Jade announced then pointed to the second man in the pictures. "But I don't know who that is."

Vahn's eyes widened as he straightened and immediately became tense. "Jesus," he practically gasped. "That's Jared Carmichael, the notorious mob boss."

Jade squinted and looked at the picture more closely. "Damn it, you're right!"

Vahn suddenly laughed and shook his head in amazement. "You got them, Jade," he announced while grinning. "You have hard evidence that both were involved in a professional hit. The pictures don't lie."

"Whoever took these pictures must have been one of Russ' clients," Jade announced. "When he was going over the client's accounts, he must have stumbled upon this."

"Perhaps he intended to blackmail the mob," Vahn remarked and eyed her. "That'd get you tossed off a twelve-story building, no questions asked."

Jade sat back in her chair and sank into thought while shaking her head. "This is big," she gasped then glanced at him. "Do you have any idea what Cody or Jared would do if they knew we had this?"

"I'm pretty sure that's where Russ and the swan dive off the twelve-story building came into play," Vahn remarked.

Jade stared at the computer screen with a strange look that quickly turned to horror. "He'd kill anyone who had it or saw it," she gasped softly then slowly sat forward while staring at the screen. "It wasn't an accident!"

"I know," Vahn replied while giving her a strange look. "We just covered that."

"No," she announced and looked at him as the color drained from her face. "No, the crash that killed my parents and my aunt. She had this evidence. Somehow they knew she had it, and they killed them for it." She then stared blankly at the screen. "She knew she was in trouble, so she hid the flash drive in her jacket and then gave her jacket to me."

"You're saying, Cody--"

Jade sneered, pulled the flash drive from the port, and sprang to her feet. "That motherfucker killed my family!"

Chapter Forty-seven

Nearly all the windows within the first-floor lobby were broken. Glass was scattered across the blood-spattered floor, and most of the lobby furniture had been trashed. A few dead gang members lay among the mess, their bodies riddled with bullets. The elevator dinged. As the elevator doors opened to the lobby, Cody's henchman fired inside, spraying the empty elevator with a barrage of bullets. He stopped when he realized it was empty.

"Damn it," Cody snarled as he walked out from behind the main desk. "What's taking Bruno so long to get that flash drive?"

"Maybe Vahn won't crack. Bruno may not be as persuasive as you think," his hired man announced. "Want me to go back upstairs and check on him?"

"No, lock out the elevator, in case Vahn got the slip on him," Cody announced while running his fingers through his bleached white hair. "We'll keep an eye on the stairs and wait for him to come to us."

The henchman approached the elevator and flipped a switch, causing the elevator alarm to sound. As he turned to leave, Jade dropped down from the elevator ceiling panel. The henchman spun to the gust of air and the soft thud of her feet hitting the floor. Jade spun into a roundhouse kick, hit him in the face, and easily took him down.

Cody heard his man striking the floor, became alert, and turned, aiming his gun at Jade. She appeared unarmed and made no motion to reach for any concealed weapons. Cody stared at her, obviously surprised that she wasn't actually dead, then frowned and shook his head.

"I should have known," he scoffed. "Were you and Vahn in on it together? Or did you con him too?"

Jade leaned against the elevator doorway while folding her arms across her chest. She didn't even attempt to defend herself. Her hatred for Cody wouldn't let her back down or run from the monster who killed her parents.

"Vahn is doing a little errand for me," she informed him, showing no emotion. "He's taking the information Greg collected on you, along with your billions, or should I say along with Carmichael's billions, to the FBI."

Cody's jaw tensed at the mention of Jared's money, but he refused to respond.

"I guess it's going to be a photo finish," she informed him. "Who'll get to you first? The FBI or Jared Carmichael? Personally, I hope it's Carmichael."

"You want to see me tortured and killed in some macabre manner?" he teased with a less than humored smirk. "That's dark, Detective."

"I've been told I lack empathy, particularly when it comes to two-bit thugs and killers," she hissed.

"I'm far from a two-bit thug," he informed her and grinned. "I've created an empire from nothing. I'm also the man pointing a gun at you, so you may want to show some respect."

She laughed while smirking. "That's not going to happen." Jade unfolded her arms and revealed a flash drive in her hand. "I found this little piece of incriminating evidence in the liner of my aunt's jacket. It must have been there for more than ten years," she informed him.

Cody stared at the flash drive in her hand and allowed her words to sink in. "Your aunt?" he remarked then nodded knowingly. "Amanda Quinn."

"You're smarter than you look," she replied.

"That's been my bargaining chip for years," he informed her then indicated the flash drive. "Do you have any idea what's on that stick?"

"Everything Russ Thomas had on you and Carmichael," she replied then raised her brows. "You remember Russ Thomas, don't you?"

Cody frowned. "Yeah, I remember Russ."

"You framed him for a double homicide then you or your men assisted him off the roof of the Strafford Hotel to make it look like suicide," Jade replied.

"I had some serious issues back then," he casually reported, almost sounding sincere.

"Then I'm sure you also remember killing my Aunt Amanda and my parents to recover this incriminating piece of evidence against you and Carmichael," she snapped hotly.

"I remember that too," he replied. "I suppose a heartfelt 'I'm sorry' won't cut it, huh?"

"For killing my aunt and my parents?" she remarked then considered the comment before shaking her head. "No, I don't think so."

His eyes then pleaded with hers in a slightly mocking manner as if they were playing some macabre game. "Are you sure you won't reconsider?" he asked then indicated the gun in his hand. "Seeing how I'm the one with a gun aimed at you."

"I was fifteen years old," she informed him. Her eyes turned hateful. "I was fifteen when you sent three thugs to my uncle's house to find this evidence."

He gave the comment some consideration then seemed to recall the incident. "You can't have hard feelings about that," Cody interjected. "Your uncle killed those men, so we're even on that one."

Her eyes narrowed while glaring at him. "My uncle never killed anyone," she insisted with an evil look in her eyes. "*I* killed your three men."

Cody stared at her a moment and appeared slightly surprised by the confession. "I'm truly sorry, for what you've been through, Detective," he announced. "Which is more than I ever got from those who ruined my childhood." His look then turned demanding. "What you hold there is key to my survival. I may not be able to stop Vahn from turning evidence against me with our money laundering and whatever else Greg had on his computer, but as long as I have Russ' blackmail to hold over Carmichael, he can't touch me. I can outrun the law; I can't outrun Carmichael." He tightened his finger on the trigger. "I'm going to ask you very nicely to hand that over. I don't want to kill you, Detective, nor do I have to. Killing you won't change anything at this point. However, if you don't hand over that flash drive, I'll be forced to kill you. Don't make me do that."

"You won't kill me," she informed him with little concern.

He stared at her then raised a curious brow and chuckled. "Are you willing to stake your life on that?"

"Actually, yes," she replied.

"I'd love to know why," he remarked then grinned. "Enlighten me, Detective."

The barrel of a semiautomatic was placed against the back of his head. Cody suddenly tensed and attempted to look behind him without turning his head. Vahn took the gun from his hand and grinned.

"Because I'm standing behind you with a gun to *your* head," he replied.

"I needed to give him enough time to sneak out the back and get the slip on you," Jade announced then casually shrugged. "It's nothing personal, Cody."

"Don't believe her," Vahn announced over his shoulder. "She wants to tear you to shreds."

Cody ignored Vahn's remark and shook his head while glaring at Jade. "I love smart women. We would have been amazing together, Detective."

Vahn chuckled at the comment. "She would have killed you in your sleep and made it look like an accident," he teased.

Cody frowned and glared at Vahn over his shoulder. He looked back at Jade. "I'm ready to discuss a plea bargain now."

Chapter Forty-eight

Miller and Jade secured Cody and his henchman in a supply closet off to the side of cubicle square. Once they were certain they were contained, she eyed Miller and raised a brow.

"Are you sure you want to take first watch?" she asked, concerned for her partner. "You should let me take a look at that bump on your head."

"It's covered," Miller casually informed her with a sly smile.

Abby approached with a cup of coffee and a first aid kit. She handed Miller the coffee and opened the medical kit.

Miller grinned at Jade. "Go get some rest."

She smiled and shook her head. "I'll relieve you in a few hours."

"Take your time," he replied cheerfully.

Jade walked across cubical square and joined Vahn in the breakroom, where he was preparing two cups of coffee. He handed her one of the cups.

"Sorry I can't offer you anything stronger," he announced and playfully frowned. "I heard there was a bottle of booze, but the geeks finished it off."

She accepted the cup of coffee and leaned against the counter. "This will do, thank you."

Vahn moved closer to her and attempted to pull her into his arms. "I was thinking once the National Guard takes over, you and I could return to your place and grab a nice, hot shower for two."

Jade set her cup down and held him back, surprising him. She stared into his eyes with a serious look. "You know what we did tonight was a mistake," she announced firmly.

"Tell me about it," he scoffed and folded his arms across his chest. "Perhaps if you relaxed a little more you would have gotten off like you were supposed to."

"No, you and me. That's the mistake," she announced with irritation. "I can't be with a man like you. I'm a detective, and you're a--"

"Glorified messenger boy currently unemployed?"

She cocked her head while glaring at him. "We both know what you are."

"People make mistakes."

"And it's my job to put those people away for those mistakes," she snapped.

"I was just helping an old friend turn his life around," Vahn informed her. "Trent did some bad things in his life. Six months ago, he told me he wanted out, but he needed my help."

"Help with what?"

"He discovered Jared was buying and selling underage girls as sex slaves. Yes, he was a trained killer, but he wanted no part of selling young girls," Vahn informed her. "I only worked for Cody, so I could help Trent find out who Jared was dealing with and help him take them down. He promised he wouldn't kill anyone if I helped him shut down Jared's operation. Cody found out about his unauthorized entry into Virtual Play, realized he had turned on him and had him killed for it."

"You were friends with a hitman?"

"No, I was friends with a fellow Marine," Vahn replied. "He saved my life overseas. When he turned to crime, I turned my back on him. When he wanted out, I agreed to help, because I owed him that much." He studied her a moment and raised his hands. "Check my criminal record. Before six months ago, I didn't have one. I'm telling you the truth. I was one hell of a soldier and a fairly unpleasant taxi driver."

She stared at him a moment then appeared uncomfortable. "I saw your record. You were a fine soldier," Jade reluctantly admitted. "It did seem strange that you suddenly turned to a life of crime, especially considering you received high praise from your boss at the cab company." She stared at him a moment. "I was surprised when he said you just quit one day."

Vahn moved closer to her, smiled, and pulled her into his arms. "I'm not a bad man," he announced. "I've never been a bad man. I just wanted to help my brother."

She stared into his eyes and held her breath a moment. "I believe you."

Vahn ran his hands along her back and toward her buttocks. "So you'll take me home with you?"

She removed his hands from her backside. "First the National Guard," Jade announced then hid her smile and sighed. "Then I'll take you home with me."

Vahn grinned then kissed her warmly but passionately. He pulled away just far enough to look into her eyes and smiled deviously.

"Don't forget to bring the handcuffs, Detective."

She smiled warmly. "Trust me; I will."

Vahn grinned and laughed.

Chapter Forty-nine

By the time morning finally came, the National Guard got the gang violence under control and worked on securing the area block by block. Cody's surviving men were placed under arrest and contained within a prison transport vehicle along with gang members and looters. Jade and Miller explained to the National Guard everything that had happened within the building since their arrival. Once the National Guard packed up and left with their transport filled with prisoners, Miller turned to Jade and sighed.

"Well, I don't know about you, but I'm heading home," he announced. "That is if I still have a home left."

"Thanks for providing backup, Miller," she announced while smiling. "I always knew you cared."

"Some backup," he muttered. "I let you get drugged, kidnapped, and chased by a front man for the mob. You're only alive because you can take care of yourself." He then hesitated and looked across the trashed office to where Vahn sat on the bullet-riddled front desk and waited for her. "And a little help from the rent-a-goon over there."

"He's not so bad," she replied.

"The jury's still out," Miller remarked then smiled. "I'll see you in the morning at the precinct briefing."

"Yeah, I'll be there."

Rafael joined Dani by what was left of her desk. She looked around with disgust and sighed.

"This place is pretty much trashed," Dani remarked then glanced at Rafael. "Do you think they'll rebuild?"

"I'm sure it was insured," he informed her. "Virtual Play can afford to rebuild."

"I wonder if there's anything left of my apartment," she remarked while scratching her head.

"Maybe we should stop by there, pick up a few things, and take you back to my place," he suggested. "It was structurally sound when I left."

"With all the looters, there's no telling what you'll return home to," she remarked.

"I actually don't live in the city, and I have a great security system," he informed her while pulling her into his arms.

Dani smiled warmly and ran her hands along his chest. "Are you sure you don't mind if I stay a few days?"

"Well, you wanted more face-to-face conversations," he teased while grinning.

"Actually, what I want most right now is a stiff drink, a hot shower, and someone to hold me while I sleep," she replied while running her hands along his chest.

"Who did you have in mind?" Rafael teased.

Dani smiled and nudged him. "Either you or Boyd. I'm not too particular."

"I'll support your decision either way."

Dani smiled and kissed him warmly on the lips. He returned the kiss then pulled away and fidgeted slightly.

"There is one small detail I failed to mention," he announced with a slight grimace. "I should probably tell you before you find out when we get to my place."

"You're not married and into threesomes, are you?" she gasped with concern.

"Oh, God, no. I mean, I was married ten years ago, but she died," he replied then managed a tiny smile. "No, it's mostly been just me and Jade against the world." He again fidgeted and turned serious. "It's just, well; ten years ago I had to take in that very pushy niece of mine after her parents died. She forced me to put my intellect to good use, and, well, I founded Virtual Play. I'm the president. I own the company, the building, and hundreds of game patents."

Larson walked past him and patted him on the back. "It's about time you confessed," he announced then grinned. "Your games were starting to bore me."

Rafael shooed Larson away then looked back at Dani. He drew a deep breath and gave a dreary sigh. "I live in this big, old ugly mansion with mean maids who never let me clean. It's pretty awful."

"You're the big boss?" she gasped then appeared stunned while staring at him. "You're *my* boss?"

"Technically, no. I'm Larson's boss," Rafael replied with a teasing smile. "He's your boss. I'd rather just repair the computers."

"You sent me the flowers?"

He appeared embarrassed. "Yes, that was me."

"That was very sweet of you."

His look turned serious. "And not because I was afraid you'd sue," he quickly announced. "I've cared for you for a long time, Dani." He looked around the disastrous office and became tense. "We need to go. I'm getting weird about wanting to clean this place even though they'll probably just demolish it."

Dani smiled lustfully while clinging to him. "I'm pretty filthy myself. I could use a good scrubbing."

"That sounds *enjoyable.*"

Dani linked onto his arm as they headed through the rubble to the shattered door.

"I have a big jetted tub in the master bath," he informed her cheerfully.

"Is there room for two?"

"I don't take up much room."

Jade watched Rafael and Dani pass through the broken door. Rafael gave Jade a sly smile along with a wave. She stared after them, hid her smile, and shook her head.

Vahn placed his arms around her from behind. "Is it just me or is Uncle Rafael getting lucky tonight?"

"I think he might be," Jade replied then became concerned. "God, I hope he doesn't call me for pointers."

"Don't worry," Vahn teased. "I think his new friend has it under control." He then hesitated. "Are you going to tell him about Cody and the car wreck?"

Jade considered the question. "Eventually," she replied. "I don't want to ruin his weekend plans."

"That's very thoughtful of you," he remarked then playfully pressed against her while kissing the back of her neck. "Are we clear to go?"

She hid her smile and enjoyed the way he pressed against her. "Unless I'm mistaken, you're halfway there already."

"Don't you worry about me," he announced. "I'm prepared to do a lot of prep work tonight."

Jade hid her smile, turned to face him, and placed her arms around his neck. "I know I'm going to regret this, but I'm ready when you are."

He pulled her against him and grinned. "Oh, yeah," he groaned softly then turned serious. "But we should probably wait until we get back to your apartment."

Jade hid her smile and kissed him warmly but passionately on the mouth. He returned the kiss then pulled away and led her from the office.

The End

Other books by Holly Copella!

Reviews left on Amazon are appreciated!

"The Battle for Andrea Maria"

A cruise ship attack turns six survivors into overnight celebrities after they take credit for the heroic act of a stowaway who died saving them.

The cruise is just what Jess needed--a bit of harmless fun far from her daily grind. But what begins as a relaxing vacation turns into a desperate fight for her life when terrorists take over the ship and start piling up bodies. Teaming up with a mysterious stowaway, Jess attempts to send out a distress call but knows they cannot wait for help to come. If she or the few remaining passengers have any hope for survival, Jess must act now. The papers dub it "The Battle for *Andrea Maria*," but to Jess it is the moment she fought side-by-side with her enigmatic Romeo, saving the ship--and losing him. She thinks the story ends there, but really, the nightmare is just beginning...

"Insanely Deadly"

When the dead return to life, it's up to an admiral's daughter and a mildly insane, former war hero to save their small town.

Jetta Cross, a Navy Admiral's daughter, is tasked with keeping her father's comrade, a former war hero turned town crazy, grounded in the real world. Capt. John Hunter is still fighting the war in his head, where imaginary dead people are part of his world. When a viral outbreak brings about a zombie uprising, Hunter is left to his own devices. He must resume his role as a one-man commando unit in order to destroy the ravenous undead. With Hunter still fighting his own inner demons as well as the undead, the townspeople fear their zombie neighbors may not be the only threat. Stranded at the island's luxurious resort with a handful of workers, Jetta is forced to live up to her father's reputation and take charge of the deteriorating situation at the hotel. She must wage her own war against the infected before the government declares her hometown a total loss.

"Deadly Institution"

A town recluse suspected of killing his wife teams up with a young woman in order to stop a killer.

After being accused of murdering his wife, Konrad Asher turns his back on the town that once adored him. Ten years later, he still holds his grudge and the title of the most feared man in town. With the reopening of the burned mental institution, where his wife had died, former employees are now murdered one-by-one, throwing suspicion back on Asher. A young local reporter, Jacey, is forced to reveal her long-time friendship with the infamous recluse in order to clear his name not only in the recent murders but to exonerate him in the death of his wife as well. Will Jacey's relationship with Asher invite the killer closer to her? Or is the killer already in her life?

"Screenplays: The Island Collection"
"Jungle Princess", "A.L.F. Resort", "Brighton Island"

Discover how romance and fun in the sun can be downright *chilling*!

"Jungle Princess" is a romantic/thriller that leaves a teenage girl stranded on an island with two male shipmates and a creature of "unknown" origin. She soon discovers the island is home to an abandoned prison with several prisoners roaming free. What really killed over one hundred prisoners? And is it still out there--?

"A.L.F. Resort" is a romantic/thriller set on an island resort with Artificial Life Forms as the main draw. At this resort, all your fantasies come true...until a malfunction removes safety inhibitors on the A.L.F.'s. Zombies, biker gangs, and mobsters run amuck, turning fantasies into nightmares. A young reporter gets more of a story than she anticipates, but will she survive long enough to write the story?

"Brighton Island" is a romantic/thriller set on a private island. When the owner's niece brings her psychic friend to the mansion, his presence awakens the spirits' tortured souls. As the psychic attempts to solve the old murders, the niece is confronted with the possibility that she's next to join the mansion ghosts. Stranded on the island with a crazed killer, her uncle wages his own war to save them. Will his "shock and awe" tactics actually save them or get them killed?

"Death Displacement"

A grief-stricken man travels back in time to seek revenge on the woman who murdered his girlfriend but inadvertently falls in love with her.

Kane is about to marry the woman he loves. His life is perfect. A few weeks before the wedding, a vindictive woman from his girlfriend's past mysteriously arrives and kills her. He learns of a traumatic accident that happened five years earlier, which triggers Riley's hatred for his girlfriend. Distraught over his girlfriend's death, Kane uses an antique time machine to travel into the past in order to find and destroy the woman responsible. When he runs into Riley's younger self, he realizes she's not the monster she later becomes, and he can't bring himself to destroy her. With a little help from his oddball friend from the past, they formulate a plan to prevent the accident that sends Riley down her destructive path. Kane's plan backfires when he falls for the younger Riley. His new tortured existence is further complicated when future Riley, his girlfriend's killer, shows up with her own devious agenda that doesn't include him. Will he be able to stop the time ripple, which ultimately ends with his girlfriend's death? Or will future Riley take him out of the timeline forever--

"Awaken the Dead"

A grieving innkeeper struggles to keep her haunted hotel out of foreclosure.

After losing her parents in a suspicious boating accident, Harley Brandon is determined to keep the family hotel out of foreclosure. Unfortunately, the hotel ghosts have other plans. Built with tainted money, the century old Horizon Hotel thrives on a tradition of murder, scandal, and suicide. As the paranormal activity increases to alarming levels, Harley discovers the truth about the hotel and its residents. Can Harley save her friends from the hotel's frightening hidden secrets?

"Dead Village"

After strange happenings isolate a small resort town from the rest of the world, nearly one hundred residents seek refuge at the closed hotel. Only eight survive the night. And that's just the beginning...

One day after the entire population of Fox Ridge Village disappears, a car wreck forces several unsuspecting crash victims to seek help at the closed summer hotel. Within the hotel, they discover the grisly aftermath of a brutal slaughter. Crash victims Vander and Devon, a reluctant clairvoyant, team up to solve the riddle of the "haunted hotel" and the mass hysteria plaguing the remaining survivors. By the time they discover the hotel's secret, they're already drawn into the hysteria. As the body count continues to climb, it's a race to isolate the source and bring everyone back to reality before they kill one another. Will Devon be able to communicate with the traumatized spirits before their fate becomes her own?

"Misfits, Inc."

A seemingly ordinary, young woman meets four misfits who claim she has given them supernatural powers.

While on a business trip to a remote island paradise, a bored secretary, Hailey, has her world turned upside down when her path collides with a psychic freak, Skyler. He attempts to convince her that they had met in his dreams, and she had chosen him as one of her four mystic warriors. After Skyler foresees a woman's death, they discover an unidentified creature has killed one of the guests. They are joined by a lounge pianist and a rich playboy, who also claim they had met her in their dreams. If Skyler's prophecies are genuine, the evil entity controlling the ravenous creatures needs to destroy Hailey to ensure its survival. Reluctantly accepting her fate, Hailey has to locate the last and most powerful of her chosen warriors, The Guardian. Their fate is in doubt when The Guardian turns out to be a self-absorbed, former cat burglar with a bad attitude. Can Hailey turn her company of misfits into an elite team of mystic warriors? Or will The Guardian's secret agenda destroy them all?

"Basement Dwellers"

A viral outbreak at a hospital leaves a mortician, sheriff, and coroner fighting for their lives against a horde of undead and the CDC.

After a massive car wreck leaves several survivors in critical condition at the local hospital, a surgeon uses experimental drugs on his critical patients and accidentally causes a zombie outbreak. When local mortician, Lexx, receives an infected corpse as her client, she becomes stranded in the hospital basement during CDC quarantine along with the local sheriff and the coroner. The infamous surgeon struggles to find a cure for his infectious blunder by using the other survivors as test subjects. Meanwhile, Lexx and the sheriff attempt to locate his missing sister, who's stranded somewhere in the battle zone that once was the emergency room. It's a race against time and the ravenous undead. Can they survive the undead before CDC sanitizes the hospital of all infection?

"Witness Protection"
Also available in audiobook!

After witnessing an execution, a resourceful young woman attempts to disappear while being pursued by a hitman and a handsome federal agent.

A helicopter pilot, Jackie Remus, reluctantly agrees to go on a date with one of her clients, but her date is unexpectedly cut short when she witnesses a man being murdered. After narrowly escaping with her life, she is placed into protective custody. When the safe house is breached, Jackie makes a daring escape from both the hired killers and the handsome FBI agent, who wants to return her to protective custody. With a little help from her sly and crafty friend, Monroe, Jackie is convinced she can disappear until the trial. While on her journey to meet with her friend, she solicits help from a few shady but lovable characters along the way. Although she manages to stay one-step ahead of the hired killers, the federal agent remains in hot pursuit. Will Jackie reach Monroe before she's captured by the FBI and returned to protective custody? Or will the hired killers silence her first?

"Town Darling"

After surviving a brutal attack that claims the lives of those she loves, a young woman seeks revenge on a corrupt town.

Going back home is never easy, but for Casey, it means returning to her corrupt hometown where she barely survived a brutal attack. Accompanied by two family friends, she seeks justice for the night that destroyed her life. Her physical scars are nothing compared to her emotional ones, forcing the local sheriff to believe that the town darling is back for revenge. As the conspiracy for her revenge appears to be leading up to the coveted town fair, the sheriff is determined to stop her from fulfilling her vengeful scheme...but guilt over his role on that fateful night continues to haunt him. Will his desperate need for Casey's forgiveness be his undoing? Or will Casey's desire for revenge destroy them both?

"Unconditional"

A young woman puts her life on hold to care for an unstable, highly skilled combat soldier, who believes someone is trying to kill him.

A botched military coup leaves a team of elite fighters injured with one clinging to life in a coma. When Harlan wakes from his coma, he's left with no memory of his past life. His commander's daughter, Indy, takes it upon herself to care for the fallen war hero. She's challenged with more than just his physical care as she combats with not only his memory loss but also his newly found desire for her. His infatuation with her becomes the least of her worries when he sinks back into his role of a combat soldier. Believing his life is in danger, his fighting skills surface, turning him into an unpredictable and dangerous man. Will his memory return to him before Indy is forced to commit him? Or will he finally find his nemesis, "the coyote", and possibly claim the life of an innocent person?

"Witness Protection 2"
The Return of Whiskey Tango Foxtrot

Believing she holds the clue to millions in missing laundered money, a young woman is placed into the protective care of a former Navy SEAL team.

Feeling sorry for her recently separated co-worker, Leeann invites Wiley to join her and her friends on their night out. Little does she know that finding her co-worker murdered is just the beginning of her nightmare. Leeann unknowingly holds the key to fifty million dollars in potentially laundered mob money. With hired killers pursuing her, the FBI places her into a different kind of protective custody. Former Navy SEAL team Whiskey Tango Foxtrot reunites to keep Leeann alive at their secret hideaway. What should be an easy assignment takes an unscheduled turn when secrets, lies, and betrayal threaten to derail their mission. Is the team prepared for a war on their own doorstep? Will Leeann's misguided trust endanger the lives of those sent to protect her?

"Deadly Institution 2"

When blackmail turns into murder, a young woman finds herself caught in the killer's crosshairs.

The small town of Stony Ridge is no stranger to scandal and persecution of the innocent. When a brutal killing shakes the town's prestigious country club, Jacey McMurray seeks help from a self-proclaimed vigilante, Konrad Asher. As her professional and personal worlds collide, Jacey fears the stress of the country club killings have finally taken their toll on Asher. Can a stressed out vigilante stop the killer before he strikes again?

"Witness Protection 3"
Alpha Mike Foxtrot

A helicopter pilot risks her life to help a team of retired Navy SEALs rescue two girls from a killer.

When former Navy SEAL team Whiskey Tango Foxtrot asks for a simple favor, Jackie reluctantly offers her air-taxi services. What could go wrong? What begins as a search and rescue for two girls turns into a fight for survival against a heavily armed drug cartel. Wanted by the law with the cartel in hot pursuit and their home base breached, the team is forced to call in a favor from a questionable ally. Unfortunately, their new safe house isn't what it seems. Without knowing who the real enemy is, can Jackie and the team save their young witnesses from the hands of a killer?

"Already Dead"
Supernatural Collection

From the already dead to the undead. Three supernatural tales of "things that go bump in the night".

"Bloodletting" - A vampire themed resort allows guests to *participate* in their Bloodletting Ritual to celebrate the island's legendary vampires.

"Reaper of Souls" - A young woman must outwit an evil sorcerer in order to save her brother or become one of his minions forever.

"Already Dead" - When Flight 220 crashes, ten passengers make it to an isolated island, but only one man lives to tell the lie.

"Witness Protection 4"
O-Dark-Hundred

A simple assignment turns deadly when a retired Navy SEAL team uncovers a plot to kill a notorious mob boss.

When Whiskey Tango Foxtrot embarks on a simple stalking case, they're not prepared for a trip to a private island paradise owned by an infamous mobster. With one of their own suffering from traumatic head injuries, the team is left scrambling to decide what is real or imagined. The situation escalates even further when they uncover an assassination plot where everyone is a suspect. Now targets themselves, can the team survive their trip to paradise?

"Witness Protection 5"
Outside the Wire

After suffering several casualties on their last assignment, a retired Navy SEAL team discovers their misery is just beginning.

When Whiskey Tango Foxtrot returns home after suffering a devastating loss, they're hit with even more bad news regarding the rest of their team. Their grief is cut short when they discover their names are all on the same hit list. Hunted by relentless assassins, the scattered team must decide whether to remain safely hidden or find the man who put the price on their heads. Against the wishes of her teammates, Jackie strikes out on her own in order to save a friend who wants her dead. In a kill or be killed situation, will Jackie's emotions finally betray her?

"Cemetery Stalkers"
Horror Collection

Four tales of horror from flesh eaters to bloodsuckers.

"Night Creatures" – A rescue party stranded on an abandoned cruise ship is hunted by a frightening creature.

"Ravenous" – After surviving a crash, a woman seeks refuge in a mysterious mansion with a terrifying secret.

"The Feast" – A creature on a bloody rampage terrorizes a small town.

"Cemetery Stalkers" – When 'The Reaper' stalks a cemetery, death follows.

Coming Soon!

"Castle Bloodshed"
Horror Collection

Holly Copella

ABOUT THE AUTHOR

Holly Copella has been writing since the age of twelve when her frustration at a book's poor plot drove her to author her own story. Over the last decade, she's written a number of screenplays, some of which she's now adapting into novels. Her fascination with zombies and other darker material lends an edge to her writing, which tends to lean toward horror. As a fan of Agatha Christie, she appreciates the craft of a good plot and the importance of creating significant characters.

Hailing from Pennsylvania, Copella lives in the Endless Mountains on a farm with her rescue horses and other animals. In addition to writing and reading fiction, she enjoys riding horses and traveling to Las Vegas and Disney World.

www.ingramcontent.com/pod-product-compliance
Lightning Source LLC
Chambersburg PA
CBHW061135200626
46817CB00016B/1499